Cover art by Basia Tran.

ISBN 978-1-7328833-1-4

www.hansbluedorn.com

Dear Reader,

I promised myself long ago that I would never put an introduction in a book I wrote. But here I am doing that very thing. Life is so sad, isn't it?

Why read this book:

I wrote this book to be a small but feisty story for readers on a budget. What that means is you can read this book and not spend a huge amount of time and effort doing so. This book has less than three hundred pages of widely spaced type and can be read in under two hours. No further work is necessary.

If at any point you aren't happy with your reading experience, you may come to my house and show me. If you can prove that your book has poor character development, predictable plot, or too many typos, I will refund your money with the cash I happen to have in my pocket at the time.

However, I will not refund your money if you don't like my illustrations. I drew them all myself and I like them. So there.

How to read this book:

Honestly, I'm not sure why this section is here because everybody knows how to read a book, but it seemed like I had to write it after I put in "why read this book."

This book has eighteen chapters. Each of the chapter titles, if read together, can tell you a little about what is happening in the story. It's just a little thing I put in there.

What this book is about:

The last two books I wrote were called *The Fallacy Detective* and *The Thinking Toolbox*. They taught critical thinking skills to unsuspecting teenagers.

This book is VERY different. If you read it, you will learn absolutely nothing about logical fallacies or the school subject called "logic."

This book is about friendship.

I have heard that my brain cannot picture the number one million. It's too big a number to hold inside my head and think about at one time. Just the same, I don't think I can hold in my head the total value of a friendship. There are so many days, hours, and minutes that I spend with someone that add up to a friendship. And I find each moment very valuable.

I am the person I am today because of the friends I have spent time with. I hold the value of those friendships inside me forever.

Over the course of this book, Archer and Zowie will battle dark matter, babysitters, teleporting microwave ovens, big penguin aliens, and even the author of this book just to be together as friends.

The right friends can free us to be ourselves.

I hope you enjoy.

Hans Bluedorn

1.
Look

Somewhere on this planet, there is a pile of hills. They are covered in grass and sprinkled with trees. Wandering through them is a road. At the end of the road is a subdivision. At the end of the subdivision is a house. And in a room at the back of the house—just past the babysitter on the left—are two friends, Archer and Zowie.

Archer wears aviator's goggles over thoughtful eyes. He often stands with hands in his pockets.

Zowie is small with a big smile and a mess of curly black hair. She wears a nicely fitting cardboard box shaped like a robot. It has silver ductwork on the sides for arms, red checker pieces for buttons on the front, and her short little legs shoot out the bottom.

Archer likes to plan, explore, and find new things over the next hill. But Zowie likes to look around, feel life, and find fun right where she is.

Archer and Zowie get along with each other pretty well . . . most of the time.

It's a rainy day. Archer and Zowie look out the window at the rain and imagine all the things that could be.

ARCHER

Do you ever think about the stuff people are made of? Humans are just big blobs of fat and protein and bone. All we are is a blob walking around and doing things with other blobs. Do you ever think about that? Why do we even exist?

ZOWIE

No, but I wish pepperoni grew on plants. I'd have a whole garden of it.

ARCHER

How does that relate to what I was saying?

ZOWIE

It doesn't. But what you said made me hungry for pepperoni.

ARCHER

But a pepperoni plant would go bad if you didn't keep it in the fridge.

ZOWIE

No, it would only start to go bad when you picked it, silly.

Archer heads off to the kitchen. He looks up at the micro-wave. The microwave is high up, just out of his reach on top of the refrigerator. It is an average-looking microwave—white with a clear window in the front. It has a bunch of buttons for choosing how long to cook food and a big handle for opening the door when the food is ready. Just an average microwave oven.

Archer grabs the power cord and wrestles with it, pulling it down. The microwave tilts over the edge and off the refrigerator . . . BAM!

Archer carries the microwave into the dining room, puts it on the table, and stares at it.

ZOWIE

Why are you staring at a microwave?

ARCHER

Hmmm.

ZOWIE

Are we going to be using our imaginations again?

ARCHER

Hmmm . . . maybe.

ZOWIE

You remember what happened last time?

ARCHER

Hmmm . . . maybe.

ZOWIE

We got in big trouble! That's what happened.

ARCHER

Hmm . . . oh, yeah.

ZOWIE

Oh, no. Here we go again.

Archer takes a clothes hanger, untwists it into a long wire and then bends it again into a big V. He tapes the big V to the top of the microwave, like the antennae on an old TV. He writes "TELEPORTEE" on the front in permanent marker. Then, he stands back, puts his hands on his hips, and looks satisfied.

ZOWIE

What's a Teleportee?

ARCHER

It's a one-way product-receiving device
using a traversable wormhole dilated by
exotic matter. We can order whatever we want from
Teleporter Order Catalog, and it will show up in the
Teleportee. The Teleporter Order Catalog sends stuff,
and the Teleportee receives stuff.

Archer holds up the Teleporter Order Catalog. It is a thick
notebook listing inside many handwritten items. A number
follows each item. Like:

Big Hot Pastrami Sandwich . . . 3345

Spinach and Mushroom Pizza . . . 1204

Milk . . . 2030

Soda Pop . . . 8392

Fork . . . 8943

Miniature Nuclear Reactor . . . 2934

Antimatter, 10 ounces . . . 2851

Black Hole Kit . . . 8744

German Shepherd Puppy . . . 7283

Milk Cow . . . 8830

ZOWIE

Ohhh, I'd like a big hot pastrami sandwich. That sounds good!

But Archer shakes his head and keeps paging through the Teleporter Order Catalog.

ARCHER

Blaster Gun . . . 5258.

ZOWIE

OK, but can we order the pastrami sandwich next?

ARCHER

OK, we'll do that after this. Let me enter the purchase code. Five . . . two . . .

five . . . eight. Send.

TELEPORTEE

Beep! Whrrr! Enter credit card number now.

ARCHER

Oh no! Didn't expect that. What now? My credit is terrible.

ZOWIE

I got an idea. Be back in a sec.

Zowie's little feet run out of the room with a pat pat pat. The babysitter sneezes loudly in the other room. Zowie's feet return with another pat pat pat.

ZOWIE

I found a credit card. But we should only borrow it for a minute. It's the babysitter's.

Archer enters the information on the credit card into the Teleportee's keypad and pushes "send" again.

TELEPORTEE

Beep! Whrrr! Ding!

The Teleportee becomes quiet. Its work is complete. Archer opens the door, and he and Zowie both look at what is inside.

ARCHER

Well, it worked.

ZOWIE

It looks like a Dust Buster.

ARCHER

No! It looks like a Blaster Gun. Oh wow. This thing is heavy.

ZOWIE

What are all the buttons and knobs and little things poking out of it? Maybe you should look in the manual?

ARCHER

I wonder what happens if I shoot it?

ZOWIE

You aren't sharing, you know. Can I hold it?

ARCHER

Uh-huh.

ZOWIE

You're ignoring me!

ARCHER

Uh-huh.

ZOWIE

Can we order a pastrami sandwich now? I'm hungry. Let's look at that thing after.

ARCHER

Uh-huh.

Zowie stands on her toes and clenches her little fists.

ZOWIE

Stop ignoring me!

She grabs the Blaster Gun from Archer and . . . oops, she shoots him. A blue light flashes out of the Blaster Gun. "VVVVVTTT!"

ARCHER

Ouch! That shocked me!

Archer becomes a little mad. He grabs the gun back and twists a knob on it and, "VVVVVTTT!"

ZOWIE

Hehe! Stop. That tickles.

Archer and Zowie start fighting—not so much over the gun, more with each other. Zowie pulls at the Blaster Gun and stomps on Archer's foot. Somewhere in the fight, Zowie's little finger presses the trigger of the Blaster Gun when it is pointed at the Teleportee!

"VVVVVTTT!"

There is a big flash, a bang, and the Teleportee shakes violently. Archer and Zowie stop fighting and look scared. Zowie's eyes get huge. She hides her nose inside her robot costume, peering out the top like a turtle in a shell.

ZOWIE

What's it d-d-doing?

ARCHER

Looks like it's r-r-r-receiving something n-n-n-new.

ZOWIE

Oohhh . . . is it my s-s-s-sandwich?

ARCHER

P-p-probably not. Looks b-b-bigger.

Dear reader, let me take a moment to explain how a Teleportee works.

It is based on the concept of traversable wormholes and

uses exotic matter to . . . no wait. Let's back up.

The goal of the Teleporter Order Catalog industry is to . . . no wait. Let's back up further.

Imagine all of space is a sheet of paper. So every point in the universe is found somewhere in this sheet of white multipurpose printer paper. We will call this the space-time continuum.

Now in your mind, take this sheet of paper (the space-time continuum) and crumple it up into a wad. Then put that wad into your mouth and chew on it for a minute. This roughly approximates what the Teleportee does to the universe.

While this process is a bit brutal to all of space and time, it has the advantage of putting everything in the universe very close together. But only for a moment.

Let's say Zowie wants to order a pastrami sandwich. First, she enters the four-digit purchase code into the Teleportee. Then, after the Teleportee has chewed on the universe for a moment, it creates a quantum arm that reaches from wherever it is (the dining room) across all of the now crumpled and soggy universe to the deli where the pastrami sandwich is. It grabs the sandwich fast and puts it in the Teleportee. All this happens in less than a googlebillionth of a second. Everyone else in the universe is unaware of what has been going on.

As you can imagine, a Teleportee is a delicate and temperamental device. Even a little shock to a Teleportee's machinery, such as Zowie shooting it with a Blaster Gun, might make its quantum arm want to reach across to a different part of the universe and grab a different "pastrami sandwich."

Back in the dining room, Archer and Zowie are about to see the result of this.

KERBAM!
ZOWIE

It's not my big hot pastrami sandwich!
ARCHER

It's not in the catalog at all! It's a big penguin alien!

A giant alien is standing on the overturned microwave. It has two stubby legs, flipper-like arms, a long round belly, and a giant nose reaching halfway to the ground. It looks like it is munching on lettuce.

ARCHER

Aahyy!

ZOWIE

Ahhhhhyy!

BIG PENGUIN ALIEN

OI!

The alien's lettuce goes flying.

ZOWIE

Is it going to kill us?

Zowie takes the Blaster Gun and changes the setting on the gun with a click. She points the Blaster Gun at the big penguin alien and pulls the trigger.

BLASTER GUN

VVVVVTTT!

Lots and lots of colorful bubbles fly out of it.

ARCHER

What are you doing?

ZOWIE

I *dunno*!

BIG PENGUIN ALIEN

Ack! Ack! Ack!

BLASTER GUN

VVVVVTTT!

ARCHER

You can probably stop shooting now.

ZOWIE

Can't. Trigger's stuck.

BIG PENGUIN ALIEN

Ack ack ack!

ARCHER

Something's wrong.

ZOWIE

I know. This gun is dumb!

ARCHER

No, I mean with that alien. I think it's allergic to
bubbles!

BIG PENGUIN ALIEN

Ack hack!

The alien falls to the ground with a thunk.

ARCHER

You killed it.

ZOWIE

The penguin alien's dead.

MARCIE THE BABYSITTER

What's going on in here?

ARCHER

Nothing. We're just playing a game. We're using our imaginations.

MARCIE THE BABYSITTER

Look at this mess! What is this on the floor?

ZOWIE

Probably soap, I imagine.

MARCIE THE BABYSITTER

And *this*?

ARCHER

Ummm. The microwave, I imagine.

MARCIE THE BABYSITTER

Well, if you kids can't play without making a mess, then you need to go *outside*!

ARCHER AND ZOWIE

But it's raining outside!

2.
Out

Archer and Zowie are standing on the back porch, looking out at the rain. It's coming down by the battalion, turning the ground into puddles and streams and little rivers, all headed somewhere out of sight.

Archer sits down on the porch.

He stands up and slouches over like a depressed ape.

Finally, he lies face down on the floor of the porch and lets out a groan of despair.

ARCHER

Huuuuuuuuh! I've decided life is boring. What's the
point of life, anyway? There probably isn't a point.

ZOWIE

Hey! Stop being grumpy. It's not *my* fault the bubbles
made a mess and we got kicked out. What are you
thinking about?

ARCHER

Hmm.

ZOWIE

Stop being a moody, artistic type!

Note to reader: A "moody, artistic type" is somebody who thinks a lot, is never happy with the way things are, and then gets grumpy because he hasn't had enough exercise.

ARCHER

I feel my brain turning into a liquid and oozing out my nose.

Zowie tilts her head to the side and peers over at Archer.

ZOWIE

Nope. No oozing yet.

She sticks out her arm into the rain and lets the water fill up her palm.

ZOWIE

Is the rain God peeing?

ARCHER

What?!

ZOWIE

Just wondering. Don't tell me you haven't thought about it.

Archer sits and thinks for a moment.

ARCHER

But, what about Gobi Desert? Does God not have to pee very much there?

ZOWIE

Apparently not.

ARCHER

I think your theory of God makes him very unsanitary.

Archer's chin rests on the floor of the porch and his head bobs up and down with each syllable.

ARCHER

Do you think there is extraterrestrial life somewhere else in the galaxy?

ZOWIE

Yes. No. I don't know. Please rephrase the question.

ARCHER

You know. Like aliens and monsters and stuff on other planets? I suppose all this goes back to the anthropic principle . . . and Schrodinger's Cat.

Archer climbs up off the ground and stands. He waves his arms around like two windmills.

ARCHER

Other planets outside our solar system are so far away that, according to my calculations, unless we can travel at least a million times the speed of light, we can't go to them. Which means we can't see if there is life on those planets. Like monsters and aliens and things. According to Schrodinger and his cat, this puts them in a constant state of quantum flux. There are both aliens and no aliens on all the habitable planets in the galaxy at the same time and in the same respect. Until we visit them, that is.

ZOWIE

You have a booger on your nose. Right there.

ARCHER

You didn't answer my question.

ZOWIE

The purpose of life is to eat, then poop, then sleep.

ARCHER

You don't seem interested in the secrets of the universe.

ZOWIE

Yes, I am. Just not as much as you are.

ARCHER

But *everybody* needs to be as interested as I am!

Archer looks up at the sky, beyond the roof of the porch.

ARCHER

We should probably go somewhere before Marcie finds the microwave gone.

The rain is gone now, and the sun is coming out. This is the middle of spring. Everything is bright green, and the air smells like dirt and grass and caterpillars and frogs and kids and rotted leaves and a smile.

Behind the house, the hills shoot up and the road turns into a dirt track. The track winds around back and forth through a crease in the hills and then climbs up, up, and out of sight.

Archer and Zowie walk up the track. Archer pulls the Teleportee behind in a wagon.

They climb the hill, back and forth, back and forth, not talking because it's steep. The further they go, the steeper it gets. And the steeper it gets, the harder it is for Archer to pull the wagon.

ARCHER

Hey! What are you doing?

ZOWIE

Can you pull me up the hill? It's so much easier this way. Pleeeeeease.

ARCHER

Get out of the wagon!

At the top of the hill stands an old pine tree. It is short, very wide, and flat at the top. It has branches close to the ground and shooting out to the sides.

They move closer and pass between the needles and giant pine cones and begin climbing through the thick branches, carrying the microwave between them.

They poke out of the top of the tree to reach a plywood box nailed to the top branches. They climb into the box. It is like they are sitting in a giant bird's nest with the sky all around. They wait as only a small sliver of the sun remains on the horizon.

As the sun disappears for the day, a small push of breeze blows over them. Whisssssssshhh. One of the most peaceful sounds around.

The sky turns from pink to red. Grey to black. Then the stars come out.

ZOWIE

The stars are so prrrreety! So big and far away. It feels like I can touch them.

ARCHER

Do you know which star is Pi3 Orionis?

ZOWIE

That one.

ARCHER

That's an airplane.

ZOWIE

Oh. That one.

ARCHER

That's a house.

ZOWIE

Oh. I don't know then.

ARCHER

You see Orion's constellation right there? It's supposed to be a man named Orion. See, that star is his head, and those are his feet. Those three stars in the middle, they are his belt. They point the way to Orion's shield. The star in the middle of the shield is called Pi3 Orionis.

I want to go to *that* star to see what's there. Maybe there's life or something. I don't know, something cool. I want to see. That's what I want to do tonight. Stars are the ultimate frontier.

ZOWIE

Why is poor Orion upside down?

ARCHER

He looks upside down where we live. If we lived in another
part of the world, he might be right side up. Pi3 Orionis is
twenty-six light years away from here. Or eight parsecs.
Or over two hundred and fifty trillion kilometers. Or . . .

ZOWIE

Yeah, I get the point.

ARCHER

Pi3 Orionis is a yellow star which means it's six
thousand degrees Celsius. It is considered a prime
location for planets just like Earth.

ZOWIE

Hmmm. It's a yellow star? It doesn't look yellow. I don't
like yellow.

ARCHER

But all the other known stars in the galaxy are either
too hot or too cold, too big or too small. If we went to
planets orbiting them, we would probably die in about
fifteen seconds flat!

ZOWIE

Let's go to a blue or purple star.

ARCHER

According to my calculations and research and planning,

this is the star with the best possibility of having a

planet capable of sustaining life.

ZOWIE

There are so many icky yellow things. Yellow school

buses, yellow snot, yellow teeth. Plus tons of other

things that I don't like. Yellow is gross. And if we went

to Pee Three Onions . . .

ARCHER

It's Pi3 Orionis.

ZOWIE

Everything would be yellow.

ARCHER

But the planet wouldn't be yellow, just the star. All

this doesn't matter though because we would have to

travel one million times the speed of light to get there

tonight, which is impossible.

ZOWIE

How do you figure all these things out?

ARCHER

Math.

Archer flops down to the floor of the treehouse.

ARCHER

If you need me, I'll be down here, waiting for my death.

ZOWIE

What's the matter with you?

ARCHER

Hmmmmmm.

ZOWIE

I mean it. Stop acting grumpy just 'cause you can't get what you want.

Zowie picks something off the floor of the treehouse and throws it at him. Archer pops back up with a book in his hand. He looks at the book and smiles.

ZOWIE

What now?

ARCHER

Where do you go when you want to solve a problem?

ZOWIE

I don't know. The bathroom?

ARCHER

Wuuuh? Huh? Wuuuh? No! The library.

ZOWIE

That too. Are those library books?

ARCHER

They're soggy 'cause it rained. Here, pick out a book.

Archer picks up a stack of books half as tall as himself.

Snakes of the World and What to Do About Them

Anthology of Carnivorous Plants

The Cloister and the Hearth.

Your Guide to the Solar System

Care and Training of a German Shepherd Puppy

Your Guide to Medieval Weaponry

Basic Astrophysics

Madagascar Travel Guide

Modern Treehouse Design

Zowie pulls out a picture book.

ZOWIE

Ohhhh *The Very Hungry Caterpillar*!

She sits down to read it.

ZOWIE

Book book book book booky book.

Archer sits down like Zowie and flips through the soggy chapters of *Modern Treehouse Design*. Then, he scratches his head as he looks over the edge of the treehouse. Zowie keeps reading.

ARCHER

Hmm. Interesting.

ZOWIE

Oh, look. There's an ice cream cone, a pickle, some swiss cheese, salami . . .

Archer holds *Basic Astrophysics* in one hand. He picks up a pair of binoculars from the floor of the treehouse and uses them to look at the night sky.

ZOWIE

He isn't a little caterpillar anymore. He is a big fat caterpillar now. Oohhh! I love the colors in this book.

Archer breaks off a forked stick from the tree. He fixes the stick to the floor of the treehouse. Then he sets the binoculars in the fork. They fall off. Archer tapes the binoculars to the stick. He uses half the roll of tape. He is a bit sloppy.

ZOWIE

And there, now he's a butterfly!

ARCHER

OK, we're ready.

ZOWIE

What are we doing?

ARCHER

I've built a spaceship. We're going to use antimatter to warp the space-time continuum. It will propel us across the galaxy and to Pi3 Orionis. This treehouse is the control room. But the *tree* is the engine. We control the spaceship using the Star Optical Wavelength Tracker.

Archer points to the binoculars.

ARCHER

If we keep Pi3 Orionis in the Star Tracker like this . . .

He looks through the binoculars. He lines up Pi3 Orionis to the center of the lens.

ARCHER

. . . and press "warp."

He points to the buttons on the railing that say "warp" and "stop."

ARCHER

Then, we will get to the planet in a couple of hours.

ZOWIE

Will there be elephants or giraffes there? I want to shoot something big with this thing.

Zowie waves the Blaster Gun and moves her eyebrows up and down.

ARCHER

You get to name the spaceship.

Archer hands the permanent marker to Zowie. She reaches over the side of the treehouse and writes this name on the side.

"Hungry Catpiller"

ZOWIE

I christen you Cat-piller. You will be a flying bushy tree.

Archer pushes "warp."

Ten . . . nine . . . eight . . . seven . . . six.

Fiiiive . . . foooour . . . threeeee . . . twwwo . . . *one*!

Liftoff! Both the tree and treehouse slowly rise. The trunk and roots of the tree trail behind the treehouse like a gnarly broom.

Up, up, up, they go.

Archer and Zowie look down at the lights of their sub-division far below.

Now they look to the sky as the big bald head of the moon flies by.

3.
For

Archer and Zowie have a babysitter. Her name is Marcie, and she was hired to watch them until tomorrow night. Usually, Marcie is a good babysitter. But this time she has mostly forgotten about Archer and Zowie. Marcie is a little distracted. She is supposed to be studying for a test, but she is shopping online instead.

But it's OK because Archer and Zowie can usually take care of themselves.

There are three things to know about Marcie. One, she has a cold.

MARCIE

Atchewwwww!

Two, she has a computer.

MARCIE

Ohh, thad looks nice. This webzite sure as some pretty zweet deals. I thingnk I'll order thatttttchewwwwwwww.

And three, she has a credit card.

MARCIE

Where's my credit card? Atchew! How did it get in the dining room?

Meanwhile, Archer is the captain of his ship, a treehouse flying through space at one million times the speed of light. The whole galaxy is before him, and the light of adventure is in his eye.

Crunch! Munch, munch, munch.

ARCHER

What's that noise?

ZOWIE

Carrots.

ARCHER

You brought carrots out here?

ZOWIE

See, all tidy in a ziplock bag. I stocked up on stuff when
we were in the kitchen.

ARCHER

I see.

ZOWIE

Well, there isn't much food at *my* house. Just a lot of
ingredients. Turns out, there's a ton of room left over in
this suit even after I get in it.

Zowie looks down at the cardboard robot suit she is
wearing.

ARCHER

What else do you have in there?

Zowie tucks her head inside her suit. Only her hair is
poking out. She rummages around inside. Then after a
minute, she pops out again holding a head lamp.

ZOWIE

It's pretty dark down there, but I found the head lamp.
Be back in a sec. Checking inventory. What would you
like?

She straps the head lamp around her curly hair, then
goes back in. She stands there, looking headless, her arms
drooping. Streams of light from the head lamp shine out of
the cracks.

ZOWIE

It's mostly chewing gum down here. Sorry, did you say
something?

ARCHER

Nebula.

ZOWIE

What?

Zowie's head pops out of the top of the suit.

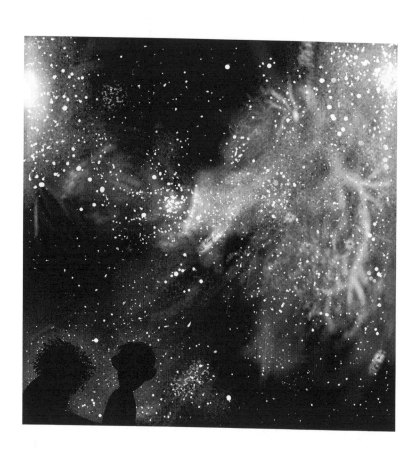

ZOWIE

Oh my! What is that?

ARCHER

We're heading into a nebula. It's a giant cloud of dust.
It's about 150 billion miles across.

ZOWIE

It looks like fire!

The nebula looks alive. It looks wise and old. It looks like it might want to kill them. It looks like it might not. It is impossible to know what a giant cloud of dust is up to.

They approach the nebula and begin to fly through it. Billowy shapes bigger than your mind can imagine reach up all around them.

ARCHER

Look, that bit of the nebula looks like a big shark.

ZOWIE

Ohhh! Now, it looks more like seafood! Or a giant without a head.

ARCHER

Oh, I can see that . . . I guess. Now, from this angle,

it looks like the giant is squishing his mom with a pitchfork. Wow, nebula, you went tragic fast.

BOOM!

Flashes of lightning and shock waves of thunder surround them as *Hungry Catpiller* moves straight into the corner of a giant billowy foot.

MOOOOOMMMMMMKKKRRR!

They are shaken around a bit as a shockwave hits them. A bunch of books fly out of the ship and drift off into space.

Kit, kit, kit, kit!

It starts to rain or what feels like rain. Maybe it's just dust. But a minute later, it clears. Archer looks into the Star Tracker and adjusts it. A big star whizzes past them like a car's headlights passing at night.

ARCHER

The gravity of planets and stars must pull us in and slow us down.

For a brief moment, they see a bright cloud as flat as a pancake. It is white-blue in the middle and gradually softened outward to a soft red. Light shoots out from the middle and straight down, like a dinner plate spinning on a pillar of light.

ARCHER

That's a proto-planetary disk. It's where planets form from gasses. See, we got pulled toward its gravity.

ZOWIE

Oh look. There's a planet!

Flash! Fzzzzzzzz!

Ahead of them, a stunning white light flashes, lighting up the entire nebula and making all its vast shapes change and grow for a moment. As they approach, a crackling and popping noise fills the little spaceship and surges through their ears.

ARCHER

It's a pulsar!

Flash! Fzzzzzzzz!

ZOWIE

What?

ARCHER

    We need to steer clear of that.

    Flash! Fzzzzzzzz!

ZOWIE

    Never eaten it, have you?

ARCHER

    What?

    Flash! Fzzzzzzzz!

ZOWIE

    What?

ARCHER

    The radiation will cook us like bacon.

    Flash! Fzzzzzzzz!

ZOWIE

    Bacon?

ARCHER

    What?

ZOWIE

What did you say?

Flash! Fzzzzzzzz!

ARCHER

What did *you* say?

ZOWIE

What?

ARCHER

What?

Archer looks into the Star Tracker and moves the controls a bit more. The ship swerves hard to the left, and they get knocked to the side. More stuff and books fly out.

They enter a cloud of full black, the darkest part of the nebula. They move through the darkness. Archer wrestles with the controls, but it doesn't seem to do anything.

ARCHER

The controls aren't responding! We've stopped!

Archer looks at the lone dial on the dashboard of the tree

house. It says "systems" and can read "good" or "bad" and anything in between like a fuel gauge on a car. Right now, it reads "bad."

ARCHER

All systems are bad!

Archer pushes the "warp" button, but they don't move. Zowie lights up her headlamp.

Their spaceship, *Hungry Catpiller,* is now an insignificant speck of light in the midst of unending dark.

ARCHER

We have to do something! We must be stuck in dark matter. Maybe it's too dense and has stopped us from moving. This is serious! I don't know how we can get loose. Science understands very little about dark matter. Maybe we're too heavy. We might have too much stuff to move through the dark matter. I'll clear out some weight.

Archer picks up some books from the floor of the treehouse and throws them out. The books slowly drift off and fold into the darkness.

ZOWIE

Stop freaking out. What did you do that for? You are
littering.

ARCHER

Ummm. Not in the vast expanse of space, you aren't.
There are googlemillions of empty square light years
out here. Nobody is ever going to see it.

ZOWIE

What are you going to do if that bangs into somebody's
face?

ARCHER

Ummm. Nothing. I won't be there.

Zowie glares at him like he is pure evil.

ARCHER

We have to do something!

Somewhere out in that depth of darkness, a small, small
light pops into existence. It grows larger, larger and then
larger. It moves closer and drifts along, tracing a shaky line
across the black.

It passes by the spaceship, stops, then moves back

toward them and rests on the railing of the tree house.

Slowly, the light dims and is replaced by a small creature about the size of a shoe but shaped like an owl. Or maybe a bug? Shaped like a cross between an owl and a bug and as big as a size ten running shoe.

It looks at each of them in turn with giant eyes. Eyes much larger than you would expect. Eyes perhaps kindly. Perhaps disapproving. Perhaps with a hint of sarcasm. Perhaps none of these.

Then abruptly, it produces from nowhere several soggy library books, dumps them back into the tree house, lights up again, and flies off into the black.

4.
That

Bump.

Bzzzzzrrrrrrr!

ARCHER

Wuuuh? What's that noise? Something is pulling us sideways.

Bzzzzzrrrrrrr!

ZOWIE

We're out of the dark matter now. We can see the stars.

Bzzzzzrrrrrrr!

ARCHER

Something is making that noise, and it's got us in a red beam of light.

Bzzzzzrrrrrrr!

ZOWIE

What's pulling us?

ARCHER

I don't know. Oh, look. The beam is coming from that thing over there. We're getting closer to it.

Bzzzzzrrrrrrr!

ZOWIE

Is it another spaceship? It looks like one.

ARCHER

I don't know. Now it looks kind of like a giant deep-sea diving helmet, but there's no head inside the window.

Bzzzzzrrrrrrr!

ZOWIE

Yeah. If it had a head, it would be a really big head.
Oh, wait. There *is* a head inside. Well, just a pair of lips
anyway. A big pair of lips.

Bzzzzzrrrrrrr!

ZOWIE

A space helmet. With lips. What does it do?

ARCHER

I don't know. Whatever it does, we can't go anywhere.
It's got us in a red tractor beam-like thingy.

Feep!

LIPS

Fifby poufanp baffobv, peef.

ARCHER

Wuh? I don't understand what it's saying at all.

ZOWIE

I think the lips just said, "Fifty thousand dollars, please."

ARCHER

How did you guess that? And, how can we hear him in

the vacuum of space?

ZOWIE

I don't know. He sounds like my baby brother.

During the Dark Ages, traveling trillions of miles across the galaxy was very difficult and took a long time. As a result, planets were not discovered, and different alien species did not meet each other. Generally, everybody was bored most of the time.

However, with the invention of the Warp Drive Engine, interstellar space travel has finally become easy. A new frontier of exploration has begun—space!

As Warp Drive Engines quickly spread through the galaxy, humans and other species travel more and more alien species come in contact with each other. This, of course, opens up new ways to make money. Such as:

ZOWIE

There's a sign on the side of the diving helmet spaceship. It says, "space tow, fifty thousand dollars."

ARCHER

Wuuuuuuh? Shouldn't that be in some sort of alien currency? Not dollars?

LIPS

Howb bun boo bipe poo pay foup bap?

ZOWIE

He wants to know how we want to pay for it. What should I tell him?

ARCHER

We don't have that much money. We're not paying for a tow. We didn't ask for it. This is an interstellar vacuum of space, not New Jersey. Besides, my mom said I wasn't supposed to talk to strangers.

ZOWIE

We can't talk to you 'cause you're strange.

LIPS

Bee bill buff pape boo bobop aff paymemp. It bill bee buufpull poo puff. Bee bill bape ipp bour pave.

ZOWIE

What? No! I'm not a robot! It's just a costume! You can't have *me* as payment! I'm not a robot!

ARCHER

What? What does he want?

ZOWIE

You can't have *me*! This is so wrong!

ARCHER

What is he saying? I can't understand what he is saying!

A cannon appears on the side of the Space Helmet Ship.
Click!

ARCHER AND ZOWIE

What?

LIPS

Pay bow bee bill *befpoy* boo!

ZOWIE

Pay you or you will destroy us? No!

LIPS

Ummm . . . ob boo fpayim *mo* poo bu paypeem bo
befpoypeem?

ARCHER

What did he say?

ZOWIE

He wants to know if we are saying "no" to the paying or the destroying. Both! Get lost, Buster!

Zowie grabs the Blaster Gun from the floor of the tree house and shoots it at the Diving Helmet Ship. VVVVVTTT!

A deafening air horn noise comes out of the Blaster Gun. Hoooooooooonnnnnk!

ARCHER

Gimme it. I'll try.

Archer grabs the Blaster Gun, twists a knob on the side, and shoots. VVVVVTTT! Pop! A little cork pops out of the end, bumps against the space helmet, and drifts away.

LIPS

Omph.

ARCHER

This gun is worthless. What are all the settings for?

ZOWIE

What are we going to do?

Somewhere out in the galaxy, there is a space bug. Her name is Patina. Patina's main occupation is wandering about. She covers vast distances in search of good food. And this is what she looks like.

With this main occupation came an occupational hazard. Sometimes, on her long journeys Patina loses track of time and gets very sleepy. She sleeps for a long time. And, with nobody to wake her up, she misses good food opportunities. Like this one.

And this one, too.

And then, BAM! She smacks into something edible. Smack!

Like many creatures get when they wake unexpectedly, this makes her both hungry *and* grumpy.

ZOWIE

Wouiiiieeee! Did you see that? A giant bug just came out of space and bumped into the Helmet Ship!

ARCHER

The tractor beam isn't holding us anymore!

ZOWIE

Woah! That giant bug just ate up the helmet ship in one bite. It sure looks grumpy. Let's go before it eats us, too.

ARCHER

We can't move very fast. The antimatter has to warm up first. Quick! Look in the Teleporter Order Catalog for something that will give us time!

ZOWIE

OK, good idea. Here, it says a Cloaking Device. What does that do?

ARCHER

Perfect. Order it. The monster is getting grumpier.

ZOWIE

OK. Wow, it's very expensive. Lucky we have a credit card number already entered. Wait, I'll enter the purchase code. There, send!

Meanwhile, back on Earth, Marcie the babysitter is still on her computer, shopping.

MARCIE

Atchew! Atchew! Ahhhhhhhhrgh! I hate colds! OK, let's see, priority shipping. I'll do that.

Click.

MARCIE

Wuh? How is that possible?

Meanwhile, back in the vast expanse of space with Archer and Zowie.

ZOWIE

It says the credit card is maxed out.

ARCHER

Wuh? How is that possible?

ZOWIE

Well, that Blaster Gun was pretty expensive. I doubt
Marcie has a high credit limit.

ARCHER

Oh yeah. That was Marcie's credit card we used. We're dead!

ZOWIE

Yup. Marcie's going to kill us!

ARCHER

No, here comes the monster!

Now, back to a living room on Earth.

MARCIE

What is this charge of $432.99 on my credit card?
I didn't order something that expensive from ...
Teleportee Deliveree, Inc. I should call.

Beep beep beep. Riiiinnnngggg!

REPRESENTATIVE

Hello. Teleportee Deliveree. How may I help you?

MARCIE

Ummm. My name is Marcie Higgins, and I'm calling about an order that was placed using my credit card.

REPRESENTATIVE

Yes. It looks like you ordered a Blaster Gun Beta at 5:34 pm for $432.99.

MARCIE

Huh?

REPRESENTATIVE

Yes. It looks like a very advanced product. But still in beta version.

MARCIE

Umm. I don't remember ordering anything today in beta version. What is that?

Definition of Beta Version:

A version of a product for people to test out before being available to the general public. A beta version of a product is likely to have some problems or bugs. Or it might have some impractical functions and abilities.

ZOWIE

This had better be a good one!

Zowie grabs the Blaster Gun, twists a knob, and shoots at the approaching monster.

VVVVVTTT! Fbbbbbt!

A small line of silly string comes out of the gun and drapes over the edge of the ship.

Zowie looks at the gun. It has two knobs on it. One knob says, "Type" and has a lot of pictures, each one a different setting. The other knob says, "Power Level 1 to 10." The power level is set at 1.

Zowie twists the power level up to 10.

ZOWIE

Come on! Zap it!

VVVVVTTT! Fbbbbbt!

Yards and yards of long, pink, silly string fly out toward the monster, covering Patina in plenty of pink ribbony goo.

ZOWIE

That didn't work.

Archer twists the ship controls. They swerve, narrowly dodging the monster and its silly string.

ARCHER

Find the zap setting again!

ZOWIE

It's out of juice. It says "Wait for recharge. Turn power setting to one for self-recharge."

Zowie puts the power level setting back to one.

ARCHER

We can't evade it for very long. Try ordering the Cloaking Device again.

ZOWIE

Oh, OK.

Beep, beep, beep, beep.
Back to Marcie on the planet Earth.

MARCIE

Beta? Oh, maybe that's my antivirus software. Hmmm. Didn't know it was that exp . . . exp . . . exp aaaaaaaaaassaaaaachewwww! I hate this cold! I'll just pay the stupid thing off!

She gets up and gets a glass of milk, takes some cold medicine, blows her nose again, and pays off her credit card online.

Click!

Meanwhile Archer and Zowie are far, far away, in the vast expanse of space.

Beeeeeptt!

ZOWIE

It's working. We're saved! Hurray!

TELEPORTEE

Brrrrrrrr zzzzzzz. Innnggggt Dingt! Buuuuurrrrrpppp!

ZOWIE

What? It's a pastrami sandwich! That's not a Cloaking Device! Stupid microwave!

Zowie slams the microwave with the side of her little fist. Bam!

TELEPORTEE

Growwwlrrrrr!

ZOWIE

Woah, this thing just growled at me. Oh, but this sandwich looks good. No wonder it cost a hundred bucks.

ARCHER

What are you doing over there?

ZOWIE

The microwave is on the fritz. Are you hungry?

ARCHER

What? I thought you were going to order the Cloaking Device! Not food!

ZOWIE

But . . . It's not my fault! This Teleportee is all messed up!

ARCHER

Can't you figure anything out yourself? I'm busy over here trying to dodge a monster in space, and you ordered food!?

ZOWIE

I'll just drive, then!

Zowie grabs the controls and jerks them hard to the left.

This makes Archer bump into the "warp" button.

They accelerate as the warp drive kicks in.

This pulls Zowie back. She pulls the controls back with her. And . . .

Look out for that *planet*!

5.
Planet!

The story so far: Instead of eating the delicious dinner which their babysitter has (forgotten to) fix for them, Archer and Zowie have been traveling at one million times the speed of light through distant reaches of the galaxy, powered only by some antimatter and a small bag of baby carrots.

The characters—current state: Archer and Zowie are currently crash landing on an unknown planet in deep, uncharted space.

The story—about to happen: Archer and Zowie are about to get very hungry. This will probably make them grumpy.

Whup whup whip!

Waaaaaaahhhhh!

Those sounds are Archer and Zowie and the spaceship *Hungry Catpiller* spinning around in circles as they enter the planet's atmosphere.

KERWHAPPPPPPPPMMMMBBPPPT!

And that's what a crash land on an unknown planet in deep, uncharted space while flying in a tree house spaceship sounds like.

ZOWIE

What are you doing?

ARCHER

Trying to start the ship again. There had better be nothing seriously busted.

ZOWIE

Where are we? Why isn't it working?

ARCHER

We are deep in uncharted space. Very dangerous. And I hope the Warp Motivator isn't busted because that would be bad.

Archer climbs out. Zowie peers over the edge after him as

he heads around to the large trailing root system of *Hungry Catpiller*, the engine.

ZOWIE

Why is that bad? This looks like a fun place. It's like home, only weirder.

Zowie climbs out herself and stands up to look around. The area is nondescript in the semidarkness. She plucks a purple fruit off of a small bush nearby.

ZOWIE

This looks good. Let's have supper.

ARCHER

Don't eat those. They could be poisonous. Stay in the ship, will you? We aren't supposed to be here.

ZOWIE

Why should I? How do you know they are poisonous?

ARCHER

You're always looking for something to eat.

ZOWIE

It wasn't my fault! I ordered the Cloaking Device, not
food! I don't know what happened!

ARCHER

Whatever. Drat! The Warp Motivator is busted. I will
need to order a new one.

ZOWIE

You're taking all the fun out of this. What are you
doing now?

Archer digs around in the control room till he finds the
Teleporter Order Catalog.

ZOWIE

Talk to me.

ARCHER

According to my calculations . . .

ZOWIE

Don't say that. You always say that. I'm getting sick
of you.

ARCHER

This is stupid!

ZOWIE

Well, if you would stop treating me crummy and ignoring me, maybe this day would be fun instead of stupid. Stupid!

ARCHER

Well, if you hadn't been thinking about food instead of what you're supposed to do. Stupid!

ZOWIE

What do you mean?

ARCHER

Why did you even have to come along? I would have had more fun alone!

Zowie is crying now.

ZOWIE

I hate you.

ARCHER

OK, whatever. I'm going to order a new part.

ZOWIE

Come back here. Stop ignoring me.

Archer is over at the Teleportee pushing buttons and pretending to ignore Zowie. Zowie approaches with steely intent.

Zowie kicks Archer in the butt.

ZOWIE

Stupid! I hate you.

Archer pretends to ignore her and keeps pushing buttons.

Zowie picks up the Teleportee with both hands and walks a couple of steps away. Archer doesn't know what to do about this, but Zowie does. With a mighty effort, Zowie throws it as far as she can, and they watch it roll down a steep hill.

Archer and Zowie look over the edge of the hill. It's actually more of a cliff. They watch the Teleportee as it bounds down, disappearing into the night.

A minute later, Zowie isn't angry anymore; she is just disappointed in herself. She sits on a rock with her head on her fists. Archer stares over the edge of the cliff.

ARCHER

Why do you have to get so mad?

ZOWIE

I can't help it. It's my natural habitat. I hated that

thing, anyway. It doesn't behave right. It's crazy. I think something's wrong with it.

Archer sits down and plays with a stick on the ground.

ARCHER

Well, until we get the Teleportee back, we can't order another Warp Motivator to replace the one that's busted. And if we can't order a Warp Motivator, we can't fix our ship. And if we can't fix our ship, we're shipwrecked on this planet. We can't get home ever. Never.

Which means, Archer and Zowie are *stranded in deep space*!

ZOWIE

I have to go to the bathroom. Getting mad makes me have to pee!

She goes away over the hill. Archer sits down on a rock, facing away, head in hands. A couple of minutes later . . .

ZOWIE

Cool! Look at this.

ARCHER

No!

ZOWIE

I mean it, this is really cool!

Archer walks over to Zowie who is looking over the edge of a cliff. Before them, the moons of the planet are rising. Not just one moon, but many, many moons are spread out across the sky. Some of them big and bright and full, some of them half full, some just a faint curve. Some of them blue, some of them red, or grey and white. The sky is lit up with a multicolored hue. But even grander than the moons, there is a thin and vast arch reaching from horizon, across the sky, to horizon, cutting right through the field of moons.

ARCHER AND ZOWIE

Woah!

ZOWIE

Look at that. It's purple! I love purple.

ARCHER

It must be the planet's ring. Just like Saturn's ring. It's

made of small rocks and space debris. It reaches all the way around the planet.

ZOWIE

Woah! What's that down there?

The light from the nighttime sky reveals the land below. It is a country of rugged mystery, covered with the outlines of mountain ranges, valleys, and canyons.

In the valley far below is a tall tower with a thin line of smoke ascending from the top. A string of faint lights, like flickering beads, are moving toward the tower.

Archer sits down next to Zowie.

ARCHER

We are a long way from home.

ZOWIE

If we look, will we be able to find the Teleportee and order the part to fix *Hungry Catpiller*?

ARCHER

Maybe. Let's try to find the Teleportee tomorrow when it's daytime, OK? I'm sorry I was hogging the Blaster Gun and wouldn't let you have it today.

ZOWIE

It's OK. I'm sorry I got mad at you so many times and called you stupid. I hate it when I get mad.

ARCHER

You get really mad.

ZOWIE

I don't like it when you ignore me like I'm not there.

ARCHER

I don't know what to say when you get mad, so I ignore you and hope you'll go away.

ZOWIE

You shouldn't ignore me, though. It makes me madder.

ARCHER

OK. I guess it doesn't seem like you care about what we're doing, sometimes. I wanted to go to Pi3 Orionis, but now we're just trying to get home.

ZOWIE

I'm sorry. I do care about what we are doing. I just need to eat or my stomach hurts. And then that's all I can think about.

ARCHER

If you promise to try not to get mad, I'll promise not to

ignore you when you *are* mad. OK?

ZOWIE

OK, deal. And we need to make sure we eat food at

regular intervals.

ARCHER

Speaking of, where's that pastrami sandwich? I'm

hungry now.

Zowie produces the submarine sandwich from inside

her suit.

ARCHER

That thing is big.

ZOWIE

I know, you eat off this end, and I'll eat off that one.

ARCHER

I don't like tomatoes. The seeds are slimy, and they

slide around on the front of my teeth.

ZOWIE

I'll eat them.

Archer and Zowie eat the sandwich. Nom. Nom. Nom.

After they eat, Archer and Zowie sit together and start to get sleepy.

ZOWIE

Are there any bears around here?

ARCHER

No. This is a different planet. There are no bears on other planets.

ZOWIE

Is there something like bears?

ARCHER

Hmmmmmm. Maybe.

ZOWIE

I can't sleep if there are bears. I heard about a guy who put on some cherry Chapstick and woke up in the morning with a bear licking his lips.

Zowie looks up at Archer.

ARCHER

Bears don't eat people. You don't have to worry. They like cherries.

ZOWIE

But I can't sleep if there might be a bear out there waiting till I doze off, and then he licks all my Chapstick off. Then my lips will be dry . . . and that's an icky feeling . . . having dry lips. I heard about a guy who got a sunburn on the roof of his mouth from lying upside down in a . . . zzzzzzz.

Archer and Zowie fall asleep in a mysterious alien land.

6.
A Lot Can Happen

Metamorphosis is a process where a creature, like a bug or a tadpole or a common household appliance, changes from one thing to something very different.

A caterpillar might eat a big dinner one night and go to bed very content with his life and the progress of his caterpillaring career. The next morning, he wakes up metamorphosed into something very different: a butterfly with big blue wings strapped to his back. This can leave the creature with a lot of questions like "Who?" "How?"

"Why?" And especially, "What is the nature of reality?"

But the caterpillar that changes into a butterfly hasn't *really* changed. Something inside him, hidden for a long time, decided it was time to wake up and show itself to the world.

Here is the Teleportee. It sits in the moonlight at the bottom of a dusty canyon. It has a few dings and scratches on it now, but it is mostly in good shape—at least on the outside.

While we can't see it, the Teleportee is now experiencing a metamorphosis.

Twitch. Twitch.

The power cord begins to move and wiggle slightly. Suddenly, it swings around and flips the entire Teleportee upright.

Now the Teleportee has metamorphosed, just like a caterpillar does. Except, not at all like a caterpillar does.

The Teleportee reaches out his power cord, digs the prongs into the dirt, and pulls himself a few feet across the ground.

Scceerrtt! Keerrt!

He keeps doing this for a while until he comes to a tree. He stares at the tree.

TELEPORTEE

What?

He continues along until he reaches a stream of water. He looks at his rippling reflection in the stream and waves his cord about in a questioning sort of way.

TELEPORTEE

Who?

He pauses for a minute and appears to think intently. Then he looks up, up at the many moons in the sky.

TELEPORTEE

Where?

He travels along through the dirt for a while past some rocks and trees.

Scceerrtt! Keerrt! Hah hah hah!

He pants with exertion. Traveling by power cord isn't easy.

TELEPORTEE

When?

Finally, He trips on a rock and rolls down a little hill and back onto his side again.

TELEPORTEE

Why!?

I know you probably haven't traveled to an alien world with all different stars and moons and a giant ring around the planet. But if on some night, you travel outside the lights of a city—if you go even further to where there are no lights at all—then you can get some feeling of what it would be like to be far out in a different corner of the galaxy.

All the stars above you will explode, each one multiplying into a thousand. There will be so many stars that you can't recognize all the ones you knew before. They get lost among this new crowd.

Stay out there all night, and the stars will turn across the sky from one side to the other.

Then, when the dawn is near, the black of night will turn to grey blue.

Below, the shadows of mountains will sharpen and grow.

The colors of the sunrise will ripple across the sky as the sun prepares to peek over the horizon.

And then, there it is, the sun.

Archer sits up. He has some gravel and sticks and leaves on his face. Next to him is a pile of cardboard and hair.

The pile of cardboard and hair sits up. Yes, it's Zowie!

ZOWIE

Go away, sun! You're shining in my eyes.

ARCHER

Ahr, my hand is asleep.

ZOWIE

Shake it around.

ARCHER

No. It hurts.

ZOWIE

Rub it.

ARCHER

No!

ZOWIE

Move it around. That's what I heard you're supposed to do.

ARCHER

Stop giving me advice!

ZOWIE

If you don't want help, stop complaining.

ARCHER

I just want you to sympathize. OK. Now it's better.

ZOWIE

I'm hungry. What are we having for breakfast?

ARCHER

How am I supposed to know? We're in deep space thousands of light years from Earth. It isn't like we can order a pizza.

ZOWIE

I don't want pizza for *breakfast*.

Brtrt!

ARCHER

What's that noise?

Brtrt!

ZOWIE

My phone is farting. It's inside my suit. Wait a sec. I'll
go in after it.

Crumple!

She wiggles her arms inside her suit and pulls out a
mobile phone.

Click.

ZOWIE

Hello?

MARCIE THE BABYSITTER

Hey! What happened to the microwave? I'm trying to
make oatmeal here, and it's gone.

ZOWIE

Um. Just a sec.

She brings the phone down and turns to Archer.

ZOWIE

It's Marcie. She wants to know what happened to the microwave. What should I tell her?

ARCHER

Well, if I knew that, a lot of our problems would be solved right now, wouldn't they?

Zowie puts the phone back up to her ear.

ZOWIE

We haven't seen it in a while. Sorry.

MARCIE

What does that mean? How can it be gone? What have you been up to? Have you been messing around in the kitchen again?

ZOWIE

We're playing outside this morning.

MARCIE

Where exactly are you?

ZOWIE

We're outside using our imaginations.

MARCIE

Oh. Just stay close to the house. And remember, you need to come inside before the sun goes down, 'cause that's when all the parents are coming back. Oh, and have you been doing anything with my credit card?

Zowie hangs up.

ARCHER

I suppose we could order breakfast with the Teleportee when we find it.

ZOWIE

Can we order a bacon and mushroom omelet?

ARCHER

Maybe.

ZOWIE

Then time to go meet breakfast.

ARCHER

You mean eat it?

ZOWIE

I say what I mean and mean what I say! But yes. We will eat it, too. After we meet it.

The sun is up for real now, and it's a good morning for a walk. Archer and Zowie walk down the hill, toward where the Teleportee had disappeared. Below them, an alien land of hills and canyons and rocks and wild savannahs all slowly slopes downward into a valley. In the middle of the valley, the tower reaches high into the sky with what appears to be smoke trailing forever upward.

Archer leads them down a steep incline into a canyon. After a few minutes of scrambling down, they reach the bottom.

They are in a field of boulders of all shapes and sizes, resting on each other in awkward attitudes. Round, squarish boulders. Boulders shaped like shark fins. Boulders with giant stubby boulder bodies, and long hawkish boulder heads.

Archer and Zowie weave their way through, over, around, and under the boulders looking for the Teleportee.

ARCHER

According to my calculations, the Teleportee should be around here somewhere. Why isn't it here?

ZOWIE

I don't know.

ARCHER

Did we go down the right canyon?

ZOWIE

I don't know.

ARCHER

We can't go back now. It's too steep. Maybe if we keep going.

ZOWIE

I don't know.

Zowie stops dead in her tracks and picks something off the ground.

ZOWIE

What's this?

ARCHER

Hmmm. It looks like one of those microwave popcorn bags. Why is it here on this planet?

ZOWIE

Dunno. What should I do with it?

ARCHER

I don't know. Leave it?

ZOWIE

I'm going to take it with us until I find a trash can.

ARCHER

Where are you going to find a trash can on this planet? If anything *lives* here, it might not even have a concept for trash.

ZOWIE

But today is trash day!

ARCHER

What?

ZOWIE

Yesterday was Monday, so today is Tuesday, which is

trash day.

ARCHER

Trash day isn't the same on other planets. That's ridiculous.

ZOWIE

No. Trash day is the same everywhere. I love trash day.

You get to see gallons and gallons of garbage moving

around in a big truck, and it goes off into the big unknown.

ARCHER

Kind of clears the mind, I guess.

7.
In The
Morning If

O n the planet Earth, where you are probably from, trash day starts with you going around the house and collecting items that you don't want anymore. From there, you put those items in big bins in your front yard. Then, a vehicle like a giant beetle drives around the neighborhood and picks up all the bins and dumps the contents in the back. From there, the trash is taken to the dump or is burnt or is picked apart and some of it recycled into other items.

The point is you never ever see your trash again. It's gone.

On the planet where Archer and Zowie are, trash day happens once a year and it starts mostly the same way as on Earth.

On that day, all the hills and canyons and valleys and streams and rivers and mountains and passes and bluffs and mesas and buttes and glens and coves and caves and potholes and all the rest of the geographical terminology fills with the locals out picking up trash.

But who are these locals?

Follow me. From where the *Hungry Catpiller* spaceship crashed, walk as straight as you can over the hills. You will find a little stream. Cross that stream and then duck under a tree and follow the other bank downstream.

Go for a while until the banks of the stream get steeper and steeper. Soon, the banks will get so high and rocky, and the space for the stream will get so narrow, you will feel like you can't get out.

Then, start looking for a big boulder. It's so big that the stream splits into two streams for a minute to pass around on both sides of the boulder. Climb on top of that boulder. It's not as hard as it looks.

There on top, you will find a penguin alien.

Penguin aliens are twice as tall as you. They have stubby legs, giant belly, a round nose reaching halfway to the ground, and two open-minded and optimistic eyes.

Penguin aliens, as a general rule, take trash day very seriously. This one is no exception.

The penguin alien pops up, rubs his eyes, and stretches.

He dunks his head in the stream and shakes his hair around.

He picks up his trash pickup stick and a trash bag, ready to set out for the day, trash day.

Two minutes later, he has found his first piece of trash, a small scrap of paper. He puts it in his bag and then stretches his flipper arms to the sky.

He picks up another piece, an empty milk carton. His job is deeply satisfying. He sees a vision for the future. He picks up three more pieces all in a row: an empty soda pop bottle, a shiny silver fork, and an empty bag labeled "antimatter." He puts them all in his trash bag.

He finds a cord on the ground. It's coming around from behind a rock. He leans his giant body over and prods it with his trash pickup stick.

He grabs it and pulls.

Beep!

That's not what he expected. He stops, raises an eyebrow, then pulls it again.

Beep!

He thinks for a moment. Then determination surges up inside. He pulls it hard and gives it a long haul. Out comes a metal box at the end of the cord.

It is the Teleportee, all dusty and a little crumpled in the antenna area.

The penguin alien turns his head to the side. He pokes the object with his stick. He puts down his trash bag and stick, wraps his two flat and bendy arms around the Teleportee, and picks him up, preparing to put him into trash-bag.

The Teleportee's power cord wildly waves around and pokes him in the eye.

Beep!

The penguin alien drops the Teleportee, and he lands face down in the dirt. He leans carefully over to examine.

The Teleportee swings his power cord around and flips himself upright again. Then, he straightens his antennae and uses his cord to wipe the dust off his window, revealing two frustrated eyes. The eyes look up at the much taller penguin alien in a disapproving sort of way.

The penguin alien reaches out with his trash stick and pats the Teleportee on the top in an apologetic sort of way.

A Teleportee that has metamorphosed is a very delicate and temperamental device. If you encounter one in the wild, you may find them to be a bit strange. But I suppose anything that can crumple up the entire space-time continuum and chew on it even for a googlebillionth of a second might have some strange behaviors . . . and/or digestive problems.

The Teleportee pokes a power plug prong at the much bigger penguin alien.

TELEPORTEE

Big *thing*!

Then he scrapes over to a boulder and digs his power cord prong into the side of it. With a great effort, the Teleportee pulls himself up to the top. He sits at the top of the boulder, slightly higher and looking more content.

Then, wrapping his cord around his door handle, The Teleportee opens it and pulls out the Teleporter Order Catalog.

The Teleportee rests the book on the rock and uses his cord to flip through the pages, reading each entry very carefully.

He pushes some buttons on its front keypad.

Beep . . . Whrrr . . . Ding!

The Teleportee reaches inside and pulls out a steaming spinach and mushroom pizza, hanging off the end of his power plug. The Teleportee looks at the pizza for a moment, then throws it on the ground and goes back to the Teleporter Order Catalog, searching through the entries again.

The penguin alien, who has been standing there the whole time, blinks. He looks at the pizza on the ground, then at the Teleportee, then back at the pizza.

He doesn't know why, but he does know what.

Quickly, he scoops the pizza up with his stick and drops it neatly into his bag.

Right then, up waddles another penguin alien, who also carrying a trash bag and a trash pick-up-stick.

Both penguin aliens must know each other because they stare at the ground awkwardly and shift back and forth from foot to foot. This is how penguin aliens greet each other.

After all the small talk, Penguin Alien 2 points to the Teleportee.

Penguin Alien 1 motions for him to wait.

Beep. Whrrr. Ding!

Out comes a bag of microwave popcorn at the end of the cord.

Just like before, the Teleportee tosses it on the ground.

With some satisfaction, Penguin Alien 1 motions to the bag.

Penguin Alien 2 scoops it up and places it in his trash bag.

Then both penguin aliens stare at the ground awkwardly and shift from foot to foot with great pleasure.

8.
You Get
Up Early

If you remember, Archer and Zowie are busy looking for the Teleportee because they were hungry and wanted to use it to order breakfast and to return to Earth.

This was because they had crashed their spaceship on a planet many light years from home.

This was because a giant space bug was chasing them.

This was because they were caught in some dark matter.

This was because ... etc. etc., and so on and so on, continuing back for a very long time until the beginning of the universe.

Currently, Archer and Zowie are on the edge of a narrow ridge. It knifes down steeply into two separate canyons, one on the right and one on the left. The blue sky reaches out all around them.

ZOWIE

Why are we going so fast?

ARCHER

We need to find the Teleportee. We need to order our part to fix our ship.

ZOWIE

What's the hurry, though? Wherever the microwave is, it's not going anywhere. I don't like this. It seems dangerous. I feel like I could fall off of this ridge real easy.

ARCHER

Just come on! We need to go down into the canyon on the *left*. It's perfectly safe.

ZOWIE

No, it's not. It's all slippery and slidey, and I don't want to slide down there and not be able to get out. Let's go down to the canyon on the right. It looks easier.

ARCHER

No. We need to go to the canyon on the left. We just have to get down there, and that's probably where the Teleportee is.

ZOWIE

How do you know for sure?

ARCHER

That's just where it should be according to my calculations.

ZOWIE

But you just said it would be up there before.

Zowie points up the ridge to where they were before.

ARCHER

Yes, but now I made new calculations.

ZOWIE

How do you know these new calculations are better than the before ones?

ARCHER

Because I'm calculating with new data.

ZOWIE

What new data?

ARCHER

That my old calculation was wrong.

Zowie stands on her toes, clenches her little fists, and shakes them behind her.

ZOWIE

I think your calculations are *dumb*!

ARCHER

Hush! I hear something. There's something down in the
canyon on the right. I can't see it, but I hear something.

ZOWIE

Is it a bear?

ARCHER

It won't be a bear. We are on a different planet,

remember. Bears aren't on other planets.

ZOWIE

How do you know? Bears are really big and smart. They

can get anywhere and claw things up.

ARCHER

No. I hear something . . . electronic.

ZOWIE

Electronic?

Beep. Whrrr. Ding!

ARCHER

I think I recognize that sound.

Archer and Zowie scramble down to the canyon on the right.

ARCHER AND ZOWIE

Penguin aliens!

ZOWIE

Just like the one we teleported. There's two of them, and they have trash bags. I told you it was trash day.

ARCHER

What are they standing around?

ARCHER AND ZOWIE

It's the Teleportee!

ARCHER

Dang it! The penguin aliens have our Teleportee and are ordering stuff with it. The credit card number must still be in the Teleportee's memory.

ZOWIE

Good. I'm going to order my bacon and mushroom omelet.

ARCHER

No, wait a minute. Something isn't right.

ZOWIE

No, I ain't scared of no penguin aliens! Hey you. That thing is ours. Let me at it. Yeah, you heard me. I'm going to order my bacon and mushroom omelet with it. Ouch!

The Teleportee pokes Zowie in the eye with his power plug.

ARCHER

Oh no! The Teleportee must have become self-aware when you shot it with the Blaster Gun. I thought this might happen. Teleportees have very delicate and complicated electronics.

With one prong, the Teleportee taps a corner of his box and contemplates his very short life. His early memories are foggy, but he remembers some things:

1. Being shot at by a small girl named Zowie

2. Being used by a small girl named Zowie to order a pastrami sandwich

3. Being kicked in the face by a small girl named Zowie

4. Being thrown over the edge of a cliff by the same Zowie Girl

The Teleportee sees a trend or pattern. But what to do about it? The Teleportee's mind considers the options.

Option 1: Avoid the Zowie Girl.

Option 2: Destroy the Zowie Girl.

The Teleportee points his power plug at Zowie and then jabs it at a trash bag carried by a penguin alien.

TELEPORTEE

Zowie Girl, trash!

That penguin alien shuffles over to Zowie and grabs her by the cardboard suit, picking her up and intending on putting her in his trash bag. Zowie wiggles and squirms.

ZOWIE

Woah! Lookout! Don't pick me up, you penguin alien!
The Teleportee's gone nuts.

TELEPORTEE

Throw away *selfish*!

ZOWIE

I'm not selfish! He's calling me selfish!

The Teleportee reaches up and pokes the air, making several invisible bullet points.

TELEPORTEE

Dumb . . . selfish . . . stubborn . . . trash!

ZOWIE

What? You can't throw me in the trash. I'm not trash! Put me down, you giant penguin alien. Stop pulling my foot!

ARCHER

I'm pulling your foot. These penguin aliens sure have a strong grip, but I think I can wiggle you loose.

Penguin aliens have short slippery hair. Archer pulls hard, and Zowie slips out of the grip of the penguin alien.

ARCHER

OK, I got you away from the penguin alien. Now, we need to get out of here. Let's climb back up the side of the canyon.

ZOWIE

That Teleportee is bonkers! Let's climb back up to the ridge.

They scramble back up the side of the canyon.

ARCHER

Phew! I don't think they can climb up here after us. Lookout! The ground is very loose up here! We are going to slide over to the canyon on the left side!

ZOWIE

The left side canyon is much, much steeper!

ARCHER AND ZOWIE

Ahhhh!

Archer and Zowie fall over into the canyon on the *left*!

9.
The Hans

In a canyon, like the one Archer and Zowie have just fallen into, the sun only shines part of the day. In the morning, it's hiding behind one steep side, and in the afternoon, it hides behind the other side. The sun only shines directly into the canyon for a few minutes in the middle of the day.

The plants and animals in a deep canyon live in the cool pleasant air. They know that they won't see much of the sun and are apparently OK with it. They live a quiet life and can't see where they are in the big universe. They just know the canyon and a small bit of sky above.

Like the creatures in the canyon, Zowie also doesn't

know who she is or where she fits into the big universe.

Archer and Zowie sit at the bottom of the canyon and check to see if they are OK.

ZOWIE

OK. I need to process this. What did the Teleportee say about me? Am I selfish? Everybody else gets hungry, but they don't tell, and then people are hangry—which is hungry and angry at the same time—but nobody admits it. But, I can't ignore what my body is doing. That doesn't make me selfish. I'm not dumb. I can do plenty of smart things. Why did he call me stubborn? I only hit him and threw him over the cliff, but I didn't know he was an alive Teleportee back then. And I'm *not* trash. Why did that penguin alien try to put me in the trash bag? I don't think I look like trash. Why is he obeying the Teleportee? I'm moving around, and everybody knows that you can't throw something in the garbage that's moving because it would climb back out and punch you in the face for throwing it away. Are you listening to me?

ARCHER

I can't resolve your problems of personal identity.

Archer is lying facedown on the ground with his arms spread out across the dirt.

Archer knows where he is in the big universe. He just isn't sure he wants to be there.

ZOWIE

Why are you lying flat on the ground?

ARCHER

Sometimes when you're grumpy, it's best to embrace it.

ZOWIE

You're grumpy at the ground?

ARCHER

No. I'm grumpy at the world. I'm grabbing it and
shaking it till it stops acting dumb.

ZOWIE

You look like a plane crash.

ARCHER

Nothing I do ever works.

ZOWIE

Can't you ever be happy where you are?

ARCHER

How is that possible? Are *you* happy where you are?

ZOWIE

Not right now. I'm super hungry and mad at the Teleportee. But, yes, usually.

ARCHER

That is so weird.

ZOWIE

What are we having for breakfast?

ARCHER

I'm not hungry.

ZOWIE

If I don't eat soon, I'm going to get all gurgly in my stomach. Then I get grumpy.

ARCHER

Oh, you do? Really?

ZOWIE

Hey! What does that mean?

Thunk!

A knobby brown nut falls out of the bush next to them and plunks on the ground. Zowie looks up to see where it came from.

ZOWIE

I'm going to eat that.

ARCHER

Whatever.

ZOWIE

I thought you said everything was poisonous.

ARCHER

It probably is.

ZOWIE

Well, I'm not going to be a pessimist this morning.

Zowie picks up a big rock and gives the shell a whack. It cracks open. She reaches in and pulls out a nut, about the shape of a walnut. She pops it into her mouth and chews.

ZOWIE

Hmmmmm! It tastes like a walnut and a carrot. At the same time.

Archer's stomach gurgles.

ZOWIE

Knew you were hungry! Here, I'll crack another one. Eat this one.

ARCHER

Oh, not too bad.

Zowie cracks more nuts that are on the ground, and they both eat them. Both are busy about the task of cracking and eating. Zowie isn't grumpy anymore, and Archer has forgotten about the meaning of life for a moment.

ARCHER

Did you know you can never see your entire self?

ZOWIE

Huh?

ARCHER

You can't see all of you. It's not physically possible.

ZOWIE

That's what mirrors do.

ARCHER

But that's a reflection. You in reverse. Not really you.

ZOWIE

Double mirrors.

ARCHER

Still just a reflection. Not you.

ZOWIE

Yes, it . . . oh, I can see part of my nose . . . here.

Zowie touches her nose with her finger. Then, she crosses her eyes, rolls them around, and looks at her hands and body.

ZOWIE

Yup, you're right. What does my whole body look like to you?

ARCHER

But you see, if I tell you how I think you look, then that is just my interpretation. You still can't see all of yourself.

Zowie sits and thinks for a little bit.

ZOWIE

You come up with the weirdest stuff. Oh yeah! I had a really weird dream last night. There was this humongous war going on over a big gold egg. And nobody knew where it was, but everybody wanted it 'cause it had power. So anyway, we went and found the egg and opened it up and out came this little bug creature. He seemed so small and sad, and he told us a story about him and Selmar Blowbeep, who was the girl he loved. And he was really sad. When he was done we looked up, and the war had stopped because everybody was around this little bug listening to his story of Selmar Blowbeep. And afterward nobody could remember why we were fighting, so we all decided to stop.

ARCHER

I'm not sure how to reply to all of that.

ZOWIE

You don't have to. Just listen. I also had a dream I was eating really good cookies.

ARCHER

Can I have another nut?

ZOWIE

You ate it already?

ARCHER

Ate what?

ZOWIE

The one I just cracked and set out for you.

ARCHER

You didn't set one out.

ZOWIE

Yes, I did. It's rig . . . where did it go?

ARCHER

It's over here.

ZOWIE

How did it get over there?

ARCHER

Ummmmmm. Zowie! Are you sure these are nuts? I

think they can move.

ZOWIE

What? Huh? What!

Archer goes over to examine one of the nuts. It's the same as before, except now, eight little legs reach out from the sides of the nut and move about, propelling it across the ground.

Zowie wipes her tongue off and spits. Archer's eyes get really big.

ZOWIE

What are they?

ARCHER

They're like walnuts with legs! It was your idea to eat the walnuts with legs!

ZOWIE

They taste a little more like carrots.

ARCHER

But with legs!

ZOWIE

We've eaten like ten of them . . . each.

ARCHER

That's eating like eighty legs. I've eaten eighty legs!

ZOWIE

You liked them when they didn't have legs.

ARCHER

Then I found out they had legs!

ZOWIE

People in China eat bugs for dessert.

ARCHER

We're not in China!

Archer stares for a minute at one of the leggy nuts on the ground. He picks it up and cuts the legs off with a rock, cracks it, then pops it in his mouth.

Zowie goes over, picks another up, examines it, picks off the legs, cracks it, and pops it in her mouth.

ZOWIE

Still tastes good. And I'm still hungry.

ARCHER

Let's put a bunch inside your suit, so we can eat them for lunch.

ZOWIE

What? No way. And have them crawling around inside my underwear all day?

ARCHER

Good point. I guess we'll have to go out to eat somewhere for lunch. Well, I think we should get out of here. I want to get away from the memory of all the legs I just ate.

ZOWIE

Where?

ARCHER

I don't know. We can't climb up the sides of this canyon again. It's way too steep. And it's too steep to go upstream in the canyon, too. But it looks like we can go downstream in the canyon, so that's our only option at this point.

The bottom of the canyon is sandy. They continue, scrambling down little dry waterfalls where the water sometimes flows. The canyon gets narrower, the rock walls get steeper and smoother. Now, they can reach out and touch both walls with their arms.

The sky is gone, covered up by the canyon. The walls are pale, rippling, and smooth. They reach high and bend over them. They walk down a little ways, turn a corner, and suddenly the canyon narrows to a sliver of a crack and goes straight down.

ARCHER

I guess we've got to go down there.

ZOWIE

Where is this going?

ARCHER

I have no idea. But they say that if you're lost, always head downstream and you'll eventually get *somewhere.*

ZOWIE

Are we lost?

ARCHER

I don't think we're technically lost if we know which way to go right now. Right?

Archer sticks his legs into the crack and begins to work his way down.

ARCHER

Hey! There's a rope here. Oh nice, the rope goes down, and I can hang onto it while I slide dow . . . ouch!

ZOWIE

What happened?

ARCHER

I've pinched a part of my anatomy.

ZOWIE

Which part?

ARCHER

It's a part I don't want to talk about. Oh, that's better.

ZOWIE

OK, here I come.

Zowie begins to squirm down. They both squirm down the crack. Zowie is above Archer. A minute later . . .

ZOWIE

I'm stuck.

ARCHER

Is it you or your costume that's got stuck?

ZOWIE

My costume's stuck.

ARCHER

You're going to have to crumple it to get through.

ZOWIE

What?

ARCHER

I said you're going to have to squish it a little bit.

ZOWIE

No. I'm just going to jump up and down till it gets through.

ARCHER

Ahh. Your dumping sand on my head!

ZOWIE

It's working. I'm squishing.

ARCHER

Ahh! Sand has been dumped on my head! That's the end of the rope. I guess I can keep wiggling. The rope wasn't much use anyway. It's getting a little narrower in this bit. It's hard to squeeze through this rock. We're getting in touch with our basic primal selves today.

ZOWIE

What?

ARCHER

I said, today we're getting in touch with our prehistoric,

ancient selves, becoming one with natur . . . your foot is on my face!

ZOWIE

Well, you're going so slow I keep bumping into you.

ARCHER

It's hard to wiggle when various body parts are getting in the wa . . .

Splash!

ARCHER

I just fell in some water.

ZOWIE

What? Where's the water?

ARCHER

Um. Down.

Gravity, as you probably already know, is a force of nature pulling everything down. If gravity didn't exist, we and everything around us would all fall up and get tangled in the light fixtures and drapery. At least, that is what very smart scientists think would happen, but they don't *really* know.

A little-known fact is that if you stood on your head, gravity would pull you up and not down. That is because, for you, down would be up. Gravity can be a bit confusing.

The subject of gravity gets even more confusing when we observe that the moon, the one we have zipping around Earth all the time, is also pulling us. But the moon is pulling us up toward the sky.

However, the moon is so small compared to the Earth that it doesn't pull us very much. It pulls us just enough to lift our hair up a little and give it some bounce. Without the moon, our hair would lie flat on our heads like a wet towel and not look very nice.

On this planet, there are many moons plus a big ring around it.

When all these items (moons and rings and stuff) align perfectly, gravity can do some strange things on the surface of the planet.

Everyone, be it penguin aliens or visiting humans, gets gently pulled toward one specific spot. The pull is very subtle, and nobody notices it is happening.

But, one day a year, everyone finds themselves walking

toward one spot. That day is trash day, and the spot is . . . we will probably see that spot sometime later today.

Right now, Archer and Zowie are moving down a canyon not knowing where they are headed.

ZOWIE

This water is cold! It's up to my thighs . . . it's up to my waist now . . . now it's up to my chest!

ARCHER

Yeah, it's getting deeper each time we go around a corner.

ZOWIE

I'm swimming!

ARCHER

I'm freaking out a little here. This is so cold. What if it gets deeper and deeper and we keep going around corners and I get a cramp, and we drown in the water, and something just touched me!

Archer claws and splashes the water, swimming to the side of the canyon, trying to get away from the unknown thing in the water.

ZOWIE

Right now?

ARCHER

Yeah! Let's get out of here! Keep swimming fast!

ZOWIE

Oh, ha-ha. That was me. I'm moving around a lot to keep warm.

ARCHER

I hate you. Oh, my feet have touched bottom again! I think we've reached the end of the pool. It's getting shallower. Oh, it's steep here, going uphill. Ah, that's the end of it.

ZOWIE

Look, it's brighter up ahead.

ARCHER

Yeah it looks like the end of the canyon up there. Let's check it out.

A few steps later and the canyon walls open abruptly. They scramble down a dry waterfall and step out into the light.

10.
Hunts

Dear reader, close your eyes. Relax your brain. Let it go. Try not to think about anything at all for a minute. Now, what do you see?

I see the rain falling. I'm standing beside a car next to a highway. The highway runs along the edge of a cliff. The cliff is by the sea. The sea is touching the west coast of the South Island of New Zealand. This is a very wild place. There are no towns or houses or people around for many miles. It's just me and the rain and the sea and the jungle. This is a place I have been to once.

Recently, I read somewhere that penguins live in this

area. They are called Tawaki Penguins, but I didn't see any. They are very rare. These penguins don't live on the ice like a lot of penguins do. They prefer to live in the jungle. Penguins living in the jungle is a funny thought.

What do you see?

Now, penguin aliens don't live in the jungle. They live in a kind of savannah. A savannah is a place covered in grass with just a few trees scattered around.

On this planet, the savannah has huge trees. They have massive trunks made out of twisty arms of bark and branches reaching far out over the grass. The branches are covered in leaves and giant nuts swinging around in the wind (These nuts aren't the kind of nuts that Archer and Zowie ate for breakfast. They are much, much larger).

If you stand by one of these trees and look at the closest other tree, it looks tiny because it is so far away, even though the tree itself is very large.

Penguin aliens spend a lot of time around these trees. They like them a lot.

Penguin aliens are usually an easygoing group. They are content to live their lives quietly. Eating, sleeping, and doing whatever it is penguin aliens do.

The long, tall grass of the savannah stretches out around. All is still and quiet. The sun is up higher in the sky. The ring around the planet leans out from horizon to horizon.

A gust of wind approaches. It grabs the grass and shoves it to the ground as it moves across the savannah. The wind passes by, and the grass raises back up, still again.

A penguin alien pops up out of the grass and looks around. He shakes his hair. He has wildly rabid hair that climbs up and claws out in all directions. It distinguishes him quite well.

This penguin alien's name is Hydro Wilson, and he is a friend of mine.

Hydro Wilson trots over to a giant nut tree and sits down near the trunk, under the giant canopy of leaves and nuts. He stares off over the savannah as it slopes downward. He looks up toward the mountains on the other side of the valley.

He looks down at the tower in the valley with what appears to be smoke trailing ever upward from the top. His nose raises high as he breathes in the wind of the day. He looks down at his trash bag clutched in his mitten hand. Hydro Wilson looks up in the sky and wonders why it is hot so early in the morning.

HYDRO WILSON

Oi!

It's not early in the morning. Its late in the morning. This penguin alien is late for trash day!

Quickly he grabs his stick and his trash bag. He waddles about jabbing at pieces of trash and putting them in his bag.

He has his bag a quarter full. Things aren't so bad.

He moves across the savannah with his head down and trash pickup stick at the ready, searching for trash as he goes.

Bump! His head smacks into something soft and spongey.

He looks up. It's another penguin alien's stomach.

The penguin alien is just standing there, long bendy arms by his sides. Black mitten hands on hips. Standing and waiting for him.

Hydro Wilson looks at the ground and shuffles from foot to foot awkwardly. The other penguin alien does the same, a penguin alien greeting.

Then, the new penguin alien points toward the giant ring around the planet, arching from horizon to horizon. Then at the trash bag Hydro Wilson is carrying. Then he spreads his short arms as wide as they go. Then points off into the distance, up over the hills and canyons.

PENGUIN ALIEN

For trash day. Trash. Much has been found. Over there.

Hydro Wilson looks at the ground and shuffles about from foot to foot for a minute. Thinking. Then he spreads his arms wide. Points to his trash bag. Then, off toward where the other penguin alien pointed and raises his arms.

HYDRO WILSON

A lot. Of trash. Is over that way. True?

The penguin alien shuffles to the other foot in an affirmative sort of way.

Hydro Wilson is a skeptical kind of penguin alien. He wants to see for himself, or smell for himself anyway. He raises his giant nose high in the air. The tip of his nose twitches about as he sniffs. His eyes look off into the distance toward where the penguin alien had pointed, gathering information and searching into the future. Then, mind made up, he begins trotting off in that direction.

The other penguin alien trots along behind him.

Over the next little hill and through a narrow path in the grass, Hydro Wilson trots. He stops and looks back, checking to see if the other penguin alien is behind. He is, so Hydro Wilson keeps going. The wind passes by, whipping penguin alien hair in all directions.

They head up toward the hills, into the mouth of a canyon.

Big rocks rise up as they go deeper into the canyon. Rocks of all shapes and sizes stare down at them as they pass.

Soon, the canyon gets shallower and broader, and they start to climb out of the top.

Then, before them is the *Hungry Catpiller* spaceship. About twenty penguin aliens are milling around it. They are picking up bits and pieces of the crashed wreckage and putting the pieces in their trash bags.

Hydro Wilson shuffles from foot to foot, and points.

HYDRO WILSON

Oh! Look at all the trash.

Hydro Wilson starts picking out a piece of wood. A branch. A little pile of dead leaves. A book. A pair of binoculars. He puts them all in his trash bag. Oh! His trash bag is full. It's never been full this early on trash day. Time to head off.

TELEPORTEE

Where are *you* going?

Hydro Wilson had not seen this strange moving and talking box before. He is startled, and he jumps straight up in the air. Then he circles the box and bends down to examine it more closely.

TELEPORTEE

More trash *here*!

Hydro Wilson doesn't know what to do. What is this thing? He definitely does not like it. He slowly backs away.

Bump!

Two penguin aliens are standing behind him.

Hydro Wilson turns around to greet them. He looks at the ground and shifts from foot to foot, awkw . . . the two penguin aliens interrupt his greeting. They point at the disassembled spaceship, then at his trash bag, then to his trash pickup stick. Then to his trash bag.

PENGUIN ALIENS

More. Trash. Pick up. Trash!

Hydro Wilson points to his full trash bag, then off down-hill toward the tower in the valley below them, then toward the big ring in the sky.

HYDRO WILSON

My trash bag is full. Time to go dump off trash for trash day.

The Teleportee jabs the sharp prongs of his power plug into the bottom of Hydro Wilson's trash bag. It splits open and all the trash he has picked up today falls to the ground.

TELEPORTEE

More trash *here*!

Hydro Wilson bends over to pick up the spilled trash.
Teleportee jabs a power plug prong at Hydro Wilson, poking him directly in the eye.

HYDRO WILSON

Oi!

Hydro Wilson looks at the two penguin aliens for help, but they stand about and shuffle from foot to foot, in a slightly embarrassed sort of way. But then point back at the disassembled *Hungry Catpiller*, now almost completely destroyed from the penguin aliens tearing it apart and putting it in their trash bags.

PENGUIN ALIENS
Trash there!

Hydro Wilson turns around and runs, quickly trotting off into the grass, carrying his torn and empty trash bag.

11.
By Sight

Archer and Zowie, who have just emerged dripping wet from the depths of a canyon on an alien world unknown light years from Earth, are about to encounter, perhaps, their most disturbing and moribund adventure yet.

Fbbbbbt!

ZOWIE

Oh wow. That is a big booger!

ARCHER

Ewwww! You blew your nose on the ground!

Zowie spreads her fingers apart.

ZOWIE

It's that big. I felt it in there. I just didn't know. See, look at it!

ARCHER

Right at this moment, I'm not feeling much hope for the future of humanity. What's that up ahead?

ZOWIE

It's the woods.

In front of them is a forest stretching out to block the end of the canyon. They approach it.

The moment they step into the woods, the world changes. All is quiet. All is still except for the faintest of tapping around them. Small things brush up against their noses, tickling. A feeling of ominous peace is in the air. Above them, the trees reach overhead, covering the sky with branches of a golden yellow. Small flakes of yellow filter down from the trees and onto the ground in an unending stream. Tap. Tap. Tap. On the ground. On the branches. On Archer and Zowie. A deep blanket of yellow snow-like stuff falls from the trees and covers everything.

The tree trunks are white with green, black, and red

spots. Their branches are strong but thin. The leaves are a greenish, reddish yellow. And the little golden yellow flakes keep falling and falling straight down and landing on the ground, covering the ground in a thick never-ending blanket

Archer and Zowie take a few steps through the forest, making faint muffled sounds with their feet and leaving clear tracks in the yellow stuff that are already starting to be covered up.

They are in The Forest of Yellow Snow.

Zowie holds out her hand and catches a few flakes.

ZOWIE

They're like little tiny flowers or beads or crumbs. Or something. But it looks like yellow snow. I hate yellow.

ARCHER

Ha-ha. Don't eat the yellow snow.

ZOWIE

Why?

ARCHER

Wow. I thought you would have heard that phrase before.

ZOWIE

What are you talking about? I feel like you're making fun of me.

ARCHER

It's just that snow usually is white. But when you, you know, pee on it . . .

Zowie's eyes widen, and she stares at the snow.

ZOWIE

That's so gross.

It's very quiet and muffled in the forest. The trees close in overhead and behind them. As they go deeper and deeper in, each step is harder and harder. The stuff fills Archer's shoes and Zowie's boots as they sink into the powder. Getting anywhere in the forest takes a lot of energy.

ARCHER

Ah! I've fallen in all the way up to my hip. I can't get out. I guess I'll lie down here.

ZOWIE

Don't lie down in this stuff. Ahh! Now I've done it.

ARCHER

I can't move. I have no energy.

Archer and Zowie lie on their backs in the snow and look up as the stream of yellow falls on their faces.

ARCHER

I feel like there is something here.

ZOWIE

Huh? What do you mean? Like something is watching us?

ARCHER

No. I don't know. But it's like something is here, searching. Like we are just going to run into it at some point.

ZOWIE

You aren't making any sense, Archer, you know. But it does feel a little creepy in here.

ARCHER

It's peaceful in here too, though.

ZOWIE

Yeah. Weird.

After a minute of resting, Archer and Zowie sit up and swing their arms around in the yellow fluff, fighting to stand up. Then, they continue on their way.

For many minutes, Archer and Zowie plod on through the yellow stuff. Archer leads the way, moving forward, hopefully in the same direction as they had started out in, but they can't be sure.

With each step, the forest opens up slightly in front, revealing only more trees and unending yellow.

Also, with each step, the forest closes in behind them, shutting their view off from where they had been only a few seconds before.

They keep going, lost in a small bubble of space, ever-changing but always staying the same: just tree trunks, branches, leaves, and heaps and heaps of the yellow snow-like stuff.

ARCHER

Hmmm. Maybe we should climb a tree? When we get to the top, we can see what's around this forest and see if we are going in the right direction. They did it in *The Hobbit*.

ZOWIE

Those movies were awesome! I loved Legolas!

ARCHER

Those movies were terrible. I can't believe you liked that effigy of shameless consumerism. I was talking about the book.

ZOWIE

Oh. What happened in the book?

ARCHER

Well, they were stuck in Mirkwood Forest and didn't know where they were so they climbed a tree.

ZOWIE

And, what did they see?

ARCHER

Ummm. I can't remember.

ZOWIE

I don't want to climb a stupid tree!

ARCHER

Well, then I'm going up by myself.

ZOWIE

I don't want to be left down here. It's not safe!

ARCHER

You are so impossible! I'm going up. We need to see
where we are. You stay here, and I'll be back in a minute.

Archer grabs a low branch, shaking off a coating of yellow,
and swings up on it.
Thirty seconds later . . .

ARCHER

Ow! Son of a three-toed tree frog! That stick poked me
in the back.

Fifteen seconds later . . .

ARCHER

Oh! I banged my head on this limb. These branches
are sharp. There are too many branches on this tree.
Somebody should get rid of some.

Ten seconds later . . .

ARCHER

Oh! I think I'm going to need a chiropractor adjustment
when I get home. So awkward.

Eight seconds later . . .

ZOWIE

This tree is fun. The branches are perfect for climbing.

ARCHER

Eek! You scared me! What are you doing up here?

ZOWIE

This is a fun tree.

ARCHER

I thought you weren't going to . . . never mind. I don't understand you at all.

Archer and Zowie continue to climb until their heads poke through the branches and out into the sky. The change in atmosphere between the tree's canopy and the open air is unexpected. The world below is a close, muffled quiet. The world above has a sky with an open, clear, and crisp quiet.

Archer and Zowie look up at the sky. The ring around the planet reaches from horizon to horizon, soaring across the sky. Grouped close to the ring are various moons.

ZOWIE

Look at that planet ringy thing. It's so cool. What is it made of?

ARCHER

Trash out in space.

ZOWIE

Oh, it's space trash! Is it getting bigger like over billions of years and stuff?

ARCHER

I dunno.

ZOWIE

Is it more than just space trash? Is it like people trash that got sucked out into space?

ARCHER

I dunno.

ZOWIE

It would be a cool place to put your trash on trash day. Suck it up, up, out into space and make it fly around the planet forever in a ring. Then you can look at your trash all the time, and it's really pretty 'cause it's a big ring now, ya know?

ARCHER

I dunno.

ZOWIE

You're no help.

A giant flock of birds approaches across the sky toward their tree. It circles above them. It undulates like one living entity and not a group of thousands of birds. It sways back and forth, then circles and swallows itself in a moment. Gigantic and changing shape and size in every second.

ZOWIE

Look. They have crowds of birds around here! Wow! Amazing! It's so beautiful.

ARCHER

Look at that funny looking little bird in the sky. Over there. It's not part of the rest.

ZOWIE

It looks like a little B2 bomber.

Archer and Zowie look at the tiny bird.

But the little bird gets bigger.

And bigger.

And even bigger.

Then all of a sudden it is tremendous and fills the whole sky and darkens the sun for a moment. Above them swoops a smooth grey body with soaring wings and a giant gaping mouth.

Swoop!

It gracefully scoops up the entire flock of birds in its mouth.

Phsshhhhh!

And blows a giant cloud of feathers out of a hole on its top. Archer and Zowie feel the wind as it passes overhead, nearly knocking them off their branch. And then it flies off. Zowie stares after the giant whale bird as it gets smaller and smaller.

ZOWIE

Wow.

It takes Zowie a while to process completely what she just saw. After she thinks for a few seconds, she says it again.

ZOWIE

Wow!

Then, a few more seconds later and much louder.

ZOWIE

Wow!

Then quietly to herself:

ZOWIE

It ate a big stack of birds. And it blew feathers.

Archer looks up at the disappearing flying giant whale bird, now far away and a little tiny bird again.

ARCHER

It was quite impressive.

12.
Not

Hydro Wilson travels downhill, not running anymore. He looks from side to side at the canyon. Around him is a field of boulders of all shapes and sizes. Round, squarish boulders. Boulders shaped like shark fins. Boulders with giant stubby boulder bodies and long hawkish boulder heads.

Hydro Wilson stops.

HYDRO WILSON

Oi!

He is lost. This is not the way he came before. He looks behind him. It's too steep to go back up. He keeps going downhill.

Soon he finds himself on the edge of a narrow ridge. It knifes down steeply into two separate canyons, one on the right and one on the left. The blue sky reaches out all around him.

Hydro Wilson sits down to think.

He looks down at his empty bag clutched in his mitten hand.

HYDRO WILSON

Oi!

It's not empty! There's something still in there. He reaches inside through the torn part of the bag and pulls out a pair of binoculars.

He stares at them.

He sniffs them.

He stares some more.

He tries taking a bite out of them. Nope. That's definitely a dead end. He feels a little embarrassed that he had tried.

He puts them up to his eyes.

HYDRO WILSON

Oi!

Everything is so far away! Why would someone make something to look at close stuff far away?

He turns them around and looks in the other end.

Hydro Wilson rolls his eyes, looks around to see if anybody was watching, and shifts awkwardly. He feels very embarrassed. It's for making far away stuff look closer.

He puts the binoculars to his eyes and looks over the canyons and out across the savannah.

He just sees grass and trees.

HYDRO WILSON

Oi!

It's that weird little box again. It's the Teleportee being carried on two long sticks by two penguin aliens. They're moving across the savannah. A group of about twelve penguin aliens is following, all carrying shovels.

Hydro Wilson does *not* like that little box. He stands up, still looking through the binoculars.

He puffs out his chest and lets out a penguin alien noise.

HYDRO WILSON

OI! OI! OI! OI!

Penguin aliens like to protect their territory.

Hydro Wilson takes a few steps toward the Teleportee to defend his territory.

HYDRO WILSON

Oi!

Hydro Wilson has forgotten that he was looking in binoculars.

He's walking over the edge of the cliff and falling into the canyon on the left!

ZOWIE

You know, I'm going to be getting hungry soon. You know, I don't think I want a bacon and mushroom omelet anymore. I kind of want a giant cupcake. You know . . .

ARCHER

How do we really know anything? You know we don't really know anything for sure. There is nothing certain in the universe.

ZOWIE

Are you grumpy again?

ARCHER

No.

ZOWIE

You need to stop walking so fast through the snow 'cause I'm getting tired trying to keep up with you 'cause my legs are short.

ARCHER

Well, you need to hurry up!

As they plod through the forest, a shape appears through the trees in front of them. A few steps more and the trees clear enough to reveal a giant wooden barn. It is two stories tall and reaches up through the small clearing in the trees. It is painted in a faded red and has a sloped wooden roof shaped like an A.

With no windows, it stands there giant, steady, old, quiet, oblivious to them. Like it's ignoring them.

Archer and Zowie don't say a word. They are both tired and want to go inside. On one side is a tall sliding door. Archer climbs through heaps of the yellow snow up to the door. With a great effort, Archer pulls the door to the side.

It groans and opens a crack, just large enough for both of them to squeeze through. Then, they are inside. Archer slides the door closed again.

In front of them is a wide hallway with a stone floor, wooden walls, and a series of wooden doors on one side. Halfway down the hallway, on the left, is a ladder nailed to the wall and leading up through a hole in the ceiling, apparently to a floor above.

They take a few steps down the hallway. On the wall to the right, between two doors, some words are scraped on the boards.

ZOWIE

It says, "The hans hunts by sight, not by smell." What does that mean? Who is the hans?

ARCHER

I have no idea. I don't feel like I want to meet it, though.

Archer goes over to the sliding door. Dotted here and there on all the boards of the of the barn are little holes made from knots in the wood. Archer looks through one of them into the yellow snow outside.

ARCHER

At least in here we are out of the yellow snow.

Archer begins to brush off his clothing. Zowie sits down and empties her boots. Then she hits her suit, knocking off all the yellow stuck to it and making loud slapping sounds.

ARCHER

Shhh!

ZOWIE

Why?

ARCHER

I don't know. I'm kind of creeped out in here.

Archer and Zowie sit on the cold stone floor of the barn and rest for a while, saying nothing, exhausted and discouraged.

Boom! The whole barn shakes.

ARCHER

What was that?

ZOWIE

That was so weird.

Boom! Everything shakes again.

ARCHER

That sounded closer!

ZOWIE

Shhh! I hear something. Something outside. Archer! I hear something walking around outside!

ARCHER

What? Where?

ZOWIE

Over there. On that side of the barn. I just heard something.

ARCHER

Let me look through this knothole . . . I only see yellow out there.

ZOWIE

Let me look through this other knothole . . . I don't see yellow. It's more of a black—

Zowie jumps back in horror and points at the knothole she was looking through.

ARCHER

What?

ZOWIE

An eye looked at me!

ARCHER

Oip!

ZOWIE

Oip! Something is out there!! It looked at me!

ARCHER

Oh, I hear it walking over there, where the door is!

Suddenly, the huge sliding door they came through begins to wobble.

ARCHER

Oip! Something is outside trying to open the big sliding door!

ZOWIE

Oip! Something is trying to get in the barn!

Without saying anything, Archer and Zowie quietly dash over to the ladder leading upstairs. They climb up the ladder through the opening in the ceiling and slide over. They are now in a giant loft area with a sloped roof on both sides and giant pillars in rows, all empty.

ARCHER

I can hear the door opening. Oip!

ZOWIE

And now something is walking around down there. What could be down there? Could it be the hans? The words said the hans hunts by sight, not by smell, and it saw us!

ARCHER

It's all quiet now. You look to see what's happening down there.

ZOWIE

You look!

ARCHER

No! You look. I'm scared!

ZOWIE

I'm scared, too!

ARCHER

Zowie, just be the *man* in this relationship will you!

ZOWIE

Grrrr. OK . . . there's nothing down there.

ARCHER

It's empty?

ZOWIE

Yup.

ARCHER

Are you sure you can see everywhere in the barn to see it's empty?

ZOWIE

No.

ARCHER

Try to look in the other corner over there to see if its empty over there.

ZOWIE

Look yourself!

ARCHER

Oh, It's empty. Phew!

Clump! Clump! Clump!

ZOWIE

Something's climbing the ladder!

ARCHER

Oip! Where do we hide?

ZOWIE

Are we going to get eaten by the hans?

ARCHER

Something's reaching over to feel around. Oip! It's
grabbed my foot! Hit it with a shovel!

ZOWIE

What? I don't have a shovel!

ARCHER

You're good at that sort of thing!

ZOWIE

Hey! Oh, it's got me now! Wait, here's a big board! I'll
hit it with this!

Bam!

Bam, bam. Rattle, rattle. Bam, bam! Rattle, rattle!

ZOWIE

There. I got it with the board. It's not coming up here.

ARCHER

It's very quiet down there. What's going on?

ZOWIE

Yeah. I'm not going to look.

ARCHER

OK, I will. Something just went through the door of the

barn. It's outside now. I just saw the shadow of it going out.

Archer and Zowie arm themselves with boards and quickly climb down the ladder.

ZOWIE

Is it gone? Do you think it's out there waiting for us? There's only one door to this barn, you know.

Archer and Zowie stand there and listen. No sound at all. Silence. Utter quiet. Archer goes over to the wall, near the door, and peers through a knothole.

ARCHER

I don't see anything but yellow snow and trees.

ZOWIE

You don't see the hans out there?

ARCHER

Nope.

But then, Archer flips his body around and puts his back to the wall. His hands grip the wall behind him.

ARCHER

Yup! It's out there. The hans is waiting for us. I saw it.

ZOWIE

What does it look like?

ARCHER

Tall. Black. Big eyes. That's all I could see. I think it has some kind of weapon, like a sword or something. It's over by the trees, watching the door!

ZOWIE

Oip!

ARCHER

Oip is right! We're trapped in here!

13.
By Smell

In the Forest of Yellow Snow, there is little sound. Noise is muffled by the tiny flowers of yellow falling down and covering the ground, many feet deep.

In the Forest of Yellow Snow, there are no smells, either. The flowers absorb everything, leaving no scent in the air.

But in the Forest of Yellow Snow, the hans hunts by sight, not by smell or sound.

The hans is a dark, dark creature with two giant, yellow eyes.

It is a proud and silent being, seldom seen except by its prey who never live to remember it.

The hans is beautiful and terrible.

About the size of a man, it plods through the snow day and night, searching for food. It watches its prey patiently for hours maybe days, waiting for the right moment to swoop across the snow and strike to cut it down. Afterward, it feeds slowly, pecking away at each corner of flesh with great detail and leaving only the bones to be covered by the unending yellow snow.

The hans stands, motionless and watches the door to the barn. Its black, black wings shrouded around its body.

Tap, tap, tap. The snow falls to the ground all around, lands on the hans, and covers it. Soon, only its eyes remain, forever open, forever fixed on the door to the barn.

It sees movement to the right! Its head automatically swivels to look.

It's a penguin alien walking through the woods. A penguin alien with a torn and empty trash bag and a pair of binoculars.

Penguin aliens walk with a sort of goose-stepping trot. Their heads and bodies are stiff and erect. They reach high with one straight little leg, then bring the whole foot down with a slap on the ground then repeat on the other side. Pat,

pat, pat, pat, pat, pat.

Penguin aliens have large feet. Even though their bodies are also large, they are mostly made up of air. They are light and can travel through the yellow snow easily.

Pat, pat, pat, pat, pat, pat. Hydro Wilson approaches the barn. He stops and looks up at the building in front of him.

HYDRO WILSON

Oi!

Barn. Yes. A barn.

He pats up to the door. It's open. He looks at the door, steps to the side, and looks at it again from this angle. Then, his mind made up, he turns to walk inside.

The hans's desire for food fills it with a surge of greed. Its black, black wings spread apart, tossing a layer of yellow snow in all directions and filling the forest with darkness. It raises its sword of matted black, poised to kill.

Its wings make one giant beat and launch it off the ground and into the air. It rises up and glides across the yellow snow toward the penguin alien.

Boom! The earth shakes with the clap of the black, black

wings.

Hydro Wilson gets a glimpse of something big and black and yellow appearing out of nowhere and headed his way.

HYDRO WILSON

Oi!

He jumps up and lands with one foot off-balance in the snow. He tilts back and hits the ground.

The hans didn't expect this. It didn't think this part through very much. It soars over the top of the prone penguin alien and slams into the door of the barn. Whap!

The hans lies in a crumpled heap of black and yellow and wing and sword and claw and leg and other body parts.

ZOWIE

Arrrrrrr!

ARCHER

Arrrrrrr!

Archer and Zowie pile out of the barn with boards raised and beat the crumpled black creature.

ZOWIE

There! Take that, you hans!

ARCHER

Yeah, we're not going to be lunch, you hans!

ZOWIE

Oip! It's moving a leg over here. Let 'em have it!

ARCHER

Take that!

Let's leave this ugly scene for a second. Stand up. Now follow me in your mind. We walk through the snow around the corner of the barn. Now, we are behind the barn, looking through the forest, through the trees, through the yellow slowly drifting through the air. Can you see it? It's a very slight feeling of lightness. When you look to the left or right, you can only see yellow. But when you look through the trees in this direction, you can see just a hint of blue and brown and white and other colors drifting through the air. Maybe over there is the end of the Forest of Yellow Snow. Maybe, it's not very far away at all.

Hydro Wilson stands up and brushes his body off. He is a little upset. The whole situation looked so undignified.

ZOWIE

Hey, penguin alien, how are you?

ARCHER

Hey! He has my binoculars!

Hydro Wilson looks down at Archer and Zowie. He steps to the left and looks at them again. Then, he steps to the right and looks at them from that angle.

His mind is made up. He approaches and pats Zowie and then Archer on the head.

ARCHER

Looks like we have a friend.

ZOWIE

I think he understands us. Do you understand us? What's your name?

Hydro Wilson stands and stares down and blinks.

ZOWIE

Maybe not. I wonder what he's doing in the forest. Look, his trash bag is all torn and empty.

ARCHER

Where did he get my binoculars, though? Hey! Maybe
he knows where the Teleportee is. Have you seen
the Teleportee? You know, a little box with mean,
vindictive eyes.

Nothing.

ZOWIE

And a long skinny arm with sharp pokey things at the end.

Hydro Wilson nods vigorously and shuffles about from
foot to foot awkwardly.

ARCHER

Well, he understands some stuff. Can you take us
to him?

Hydro Wilson turns around and pats off around the barn
and toward the trees, then turns around to look behind at
Archer and Zowie in a "are you coming?" sort of way.

ZOWIE

Where's he going?

ARCHER

I don't know. Maybe he's going to lead us to
the Teleportee.

ZOWIE

Should we follow him? Should we leave this crumpled
mass of hans here? Is it dead?

ARCHER

Ummm. I guess so.

They walk through the yellow snow following the giant
body of Hydro Wilson. After a few minutes, the space ahead
starts to feel a little more open and a little less yellow.

They keep walking, and soon the edge of the trees is in
sight. A few steps more, and Archer and Zowie pass the last
tree and step out of the Forest of Yellow Snow and into the
hot sun.

Before them, the savannah opens up and touches the
sky. The green and brown sea of grass leans downward and
shimmers in the sun. The trees are scattered around. Above,
puffy clouds briskly walk across the sky, getting smaller and
smaller as they head toward the horizon.

The tower that was far away before is closer at the bottom of the savannah.

ARCHER

It's hot now.

ZOWIE

Yeah. Where do we go?

ARCHER

I dunno.

But Hydro Wilson knows where he is going. He leads the way.

14.

A Big Lunch Is Eaten With Friends

If you stand under a tree, you can learn a lot. It creaks and whispers. It growls and scrapes. It bends and sways. It can tell you what the weather is now and what it will be like in a minute. It can tell you all is well with the world, and it can tell you to go inside. Sometimes it's perfectly quiet.

Sometimes I think about all the trees I have seen cut

down to leave room for something else like a house or a field of corn or a bridge or a giant tornado passing by or for really nothing at all. Sometimes I think trees care more about us than we care about them.

It's windy out, and clouds are flying around everywhere. They are moving across the sky covering and uncovering moons, rings, the sun, and things.

A little ways away are two penguin aliens gathered under a giant nut tree. This is the kind of nut tree that penguin aliens spend so much time under. This tree is larger than most. It stretches out over the savannah with shady branches. Dark green leaves and giant brown nuts cover the ends of the branches.

Archer and Zowie approach, following Hydro Wilson. They pass under the branches and enter the shade. Here, the air is cool with a feeling of peace.

The two penguin aliens are standing, shuffling from foot to foot and looking at the ground. Hydro Wilson approaches them and does the same.

Now, hanging out with penguin aliens is a little awkward. They stand about, shuffle from foot to foot. You know, do all that stuff. And that's what's happening most of the time.

ARCHER

Do you think these penguin aliens understand what we say?

ZOWIE

They seem to understand some stuff.

ARCHER

Maybe I'll tell them our situation. Hello! Our spaceship crashed here. We had a Teleportee to fix it, but it poked us in the eye instead. Now, we're wandering around trying to find it again.

ZOWIE

You aren't giving them any details! Here's what happened. We flew through this cool nebula last night and got towed and chased by a space bug and the Teleportee. He is a person now but calling me names too and poked me in the eye, and the other penguin aliens tried putting me in the trash. You guys are nice, so the Teleportee must have lied to them about me. And we ate some nuts with legs for breakfast on accident, but they were good and then we swam in a canyon and the forest with yellow snow is gross but peaceful until we got attacked by the hans. I think it's dead now.

The three penguin aliens stop shuffling and stare at Zowie.

ZOWIE

Do you think they understood me? Nobody is doing anything. They're just staring.

ARCHER

I feel your narrative style is . . . impressionistic.

ZOWIE

What does that mean? You didn't say hardly anything that happened, so I had to give details.

ARCHER

Yeah, but I feel like I've just been attacked by a Jackson Pollock painting of details.

ZOWIE

Hey!

A gust of wind whispers in the branches and leaves above. A second later it echoes below, blowing across the savannah and swirling the air about under the tree.

ZOWIE

Oh. I think it's lunchtime. They're getting something out of bags.

ARCHER

Hmm. If lunchtime on this planet is anything like breakfast, I don't want to eat whatever weird, gross thing they have.

ZOWIE

Oh, come on. You admitted breakfast was good. I wonder what they are they having for lunch. It's *sandwiches*! I'm sorry I killed one of you with bubbles. You guys are the best. Can we have some?

The penguin aliens shuffle about in a "yes" sort of way.

ZOWIE

Yay!

ARCHER

Woah, they each have stuff for making sandwiches.

It's odd that they have sandwiches on a planet

googletrillions of miles from Earth, don't you think?

ZOWIE

I don't know. Maybe sandwiches were introduced by the

Mormon pioneers or something.

ARCHER

The what?

ZOWIE

Oh, look they have meat and vegetables and . . .

like everything!

ARCHER

Oh, wow, they like making big sandwiches here.

ZOWIE

How is he going to fit that thing in his mouth?

ARCHER

I know, right? Where is his mouth, anyway?

ARCHER AND ZOWIE

Ohhhh! That's where his mouth is.

ARCHER

I just watched someone make a huge sandwich, and
now I'm starving.

ZOWIE

Well, they said we could have some. Let's get a makin'.

Archer and Zowie each make a massive sandwich, piled
high with colorful and juicy ingredients.

A few minutes later, Archer and Zowie and their new
friends settle into eating. Everyone is chewing, lost in their
thoughts.

Munch, munch, munch.

Chew, chew, chew.

Nom, nom, nom.

ZOWIE

Yummmmmy! I'm very much in touch with my lunch
right now. I made some good choices with
this sandwich.

ARCHER

I didn't know what was going to taste good, so I just put
it all on.

ZOWIE

How did it turn out?

ARCHER

Pretty good, I'd say, but also a little confusing.

Munch, munch, munch.

Chew, chew, chew.

Nom, nom, nom.

ZOWIE

You know what, Archer, eating lunch makes me think.
I've been thinking about something.

ARCHER

What?

ZOWIE

I wouldn't be afraid of a giant marshmallow man. You
know, from *Ghostbusters*. I would just grab chunks out
of his legs and eat them.

ARCHER

I'm not sure if I understand the question. Was there
a question?

ZOWIE

No, just thinking about it. You know like this. Chomp.
Chomp! Chomp!

Zowie bites big chunks out of an imaginary marshmallow leg.

ARCHER

Is he toasted first?

ZOWIE

Probably not.

Munch, munch, munch.

Chew, chew, chew.

Nom, nom, nom.

ARCHER

I've heard people say that I need to get an education
because it's the only thing people can't take away from
me. But what if I get amnesia? Then I won't remember
what I learned. Yeah, then I'm in trouble.

ZOWIE

Well, what doesn't kill you makes you stronger. Except
for bears. Bears will kill you.

ARCHER

I don't know how that relates to what I was saying.

ZOWIE

I don't know how your face relates to what I was saying.
Oh, man! That was a really good sandwich. I ate too
much food, though.

Everyone finishes eating. Then, one penguin alien stands
up. He points. He spreads his arms and waves them. He
stands still. He points again. Then he makes a square out of
his hands. Then he sits back down.

The other two penguin aliens clap their mitten hands.

ARCHER

I think that penguin alien just told a story.

ZOWIE

Yeah, you're right. Now that one is going to tell a story.
He's standing up.

ARCHER

I have no idea what this story is about. Something
about the clouds and lots of flapping.

ZOWIE

Look, they all are laughing, I think. Anyway, they look amused. I think he told a joke or something.

ARCHER

Yeah, I can see how that was funny, kind of.

ZOWIE

Oh, now our penguin alien is telling a story.

ARCHER

I think he's telling a story about the Teleportee.

ZOWIE

How do you know?

ARCHER

Look at his hands. They keep forming a box and then antennae.

ZOWIE

Oh, yeah, I see.

ARCHER

Oh, wow. It looks like he didn't have a good experience with the Teleportee.

ZOWIE

Ha, big surprise, right? Oh, it looks like story time is

over. They've stopped.

ARCHER

Um, no it's not. It's your turn.

ZOWIE

What! I don't want to tell a story. I don't have a story.

ARCHER

I think you have to. That's the way it works here.

ZOWIE

Um . . . OK. Here's my story. Once upon a time at Arby's, there was a curly fry. He was alone in the tray and missed his friends 'cause they were all eaten up, and his name was Ben. Then the Arby's guy came by and dumped a whole load of fresh curly fries on top of Ben, and now he wasn't alone anymore. But then Zowie poured horsey sauce all over the fries and gobbled them all up. The end!"

All the penguin aliens clap.

ZOWIE

Now, they're looking at you. Ha! It's your turn now.

ARCHER

Um. Once three little pigs were very bored and had

nothing to do. Then they flew into space on a rocket ship. Then they were still bored and had nothing interesting to do. Then the rocket ship blew up. And they died. The end.

ZOWIE

Your story is depressing.

ARCHER

But your story was confusing. Who is the protagonist, Ben the curly fry or Zowie?

ZOWIE

I don't know what a protagonist is.

ARCHER

It's the hero.

ZOWIE

Oh, then it's me 'cause I get to eat the curly fries.

ARCHER

It still doesn't hold to any storytelling conventions.

ZOWIE

Yes, it does. It has plenty of conventionals.

ARCHER

OK. Let's put it to a vote. Which story made more sense?

All the penguin aliens point at Zowie.

ZOWIE

Why are they staring at me now?

ARCHER

I think they liked your story and want you to tell
another one.

ZOWIE

But I don't have another story.

ARCHER

Don't you have that book?

ZOWIE

The Very Hungry Caterpillar!

Zowie wiggles, squirms, and her head disappears into
her suit. A headless Zowie tilts and shakes and bulges about
for a minute.

ZOWIE

It's wet down here, and it's starting to smell funny.

ARCHER

You should probably take the suit off.

ZOWIE

No!

Then, a soggy book, *The Very Hungry Caterpillar*, squeezes out of the head hole and falls to the ground. Another minute later, Zowie's head pops back out. She begins to read.

All three penguin aliens crowd behind her. They look over her shoulders at each of the brightly colored pictures and listen as if hypnotized. She reads about the moon and the little egg on the leaf. She reads about all the different foods the caterpillar eats. Then, she turns the last page and reads about the caterpillar eating a hole through his cocoon and busting out as a brand-new butterfly.

At that, all three penguin aliens jump back in surprise.

ALL THE PENGUIN ALIENS

Oi!

ZOWIE

Wow. I didn't think you guys would like it that much. You can have the book. It's not mine, anyway. It belongs to the library, and I don't think they want a soggy book back.

The penguin aliens take the book and hold it between themselves, turning each page as they go through it again. They point at different pages, craning over each other's heads to look.

Hydro Wilson gets up and walks over to the giant trunk of the tree. He looks up in the branches above and touches the twisted muscles of bark.

The wind blows. The giant tree whispers and shakes in a gentle sort of way.

He goes over to the nuts scattered under the giant nut tree and looks around at them for a minute. Then, he bends over and picks one up. It's about the size of a watermelon but brown and wrinkled, more brown and wrinkled than the rest. He cracks it open with his two mitten hands.

A tiny, baby penguin alien jumps out of the broken nut and runs off toward the savannah. He disappears into the grass.

Hydro Wilson walks back to the others and sits down.

The wind passes by for a minute. The tree stretches about in the wind in a grateful sort of way.

Archer and Zowie watch all this, afraid to say anything. Afraid to break the moment. They sense that they aren't a part of it, but it's OK to be there for it.

The wind blows through the tree, settling into a steady breeze. A minute passes.

ARCHER

Hmm. Our penguin alien looks pretty depressed about his trash bag.

ZOWIE

He can't pick up trash today. Oh! Wait a sec. Be back in a minute.

ARCHER

What have you got in your suit this time?

ZOWIE

Sewing kit.

A minute later . . .

ZOWIE

It's all sewed up now. All fixed! I hope you like it. I don't
know how to sew really well, but I think it will hold
trash.

Zowie reaches up to the much taller penguin alien and
hands the sewn trash bag back to Hydro Wilson. He looks at
it carefully. Examining the hole where it was stitched shut.
Then, he looks up and shuffles in a thankful sort of way.

He removes the binoculars, draped around his head, and
hands them to Archer.

ARCHER

Is this how I find the Teleportee?

Hydro Wilson shuffles about in an affirmative sort of way.

ARCHER

Thanks, guys. Thanks for everything.

ZOWIE

Yeah, thanks for the lunch. It was really good.

One by one, the penguin aliens begin to gather their trash bags and sticks. Each one pats Archer and Zowie on the head in a friendly sort of way then wanders off into the grass, looking for trash.

Hydro Wilson leaves last. He pats both on the head, stands and shuffles for a minute, then trots off.

Archer and Zowie are alone again.

15.
Zowie

Here comes the wind. This wind is wild. This wind brings change. We hide to stay out of the wind. Or we step into the wind and let it carry us around all day.

The wind is all around us now, and we are afraid.

Step into the wind and let it carry us around all day.

The tree branches above them begin to jerk about, whispering and then whistling with a shrill voice. They shudder like they are trying to say something.

A minute later, the wind catches Archer and Zowie. It cuts through to their skin with cold air, carrying with it a few drops of rain. The storm clouds that were a ways away before are directly overhead now, making everything darker.

ZOWIE

It's raining.

ARCHER

Yup. I'm looking around at this planet in my binoculars to see if I can find the Teleportee.

ZOWIE

It looks like it's gonna rain hard in a minute. The storm clouds are comin'. We need to find somewhere to go inside. I don't want to get struck by lightning.

ARCHER

What's that?

ZOWIE

What is what?

ARCHER

It's way over there. It looks like the Teleportee. It is the Teleportee!

ZOWIE

Gimme the binoculars! Yup, that's him. Look at him go, scrapin' along. He travels weird. He's all by himself. Why is he by himself? It's strange.

ARCHER

Let's go get him.

ZOWIE

It looks like he's moving pretty fast. Why isn't he around his big bad penguin alien buddies?

ARCHER

I don't know. But we should get him and order the part to fix the ship.

ZOWIE

Um. I don't like this. It's starting to rain cold. And I
don't trust that guy. He pokes stuff in the eye.

ARCHER

Come on, Zowie. If you hold the cord, I'll order the part.
I don't think he can do anything without his cord. We
need to get him now. It's our only chance before he
goes off and we lose him in the grass.

ZOWIE

OK.

Zowie and Archer step out of the shelter of the tree and
into the wind. Above them, the tree bends hard to the side,
lifting the branches to grasp at the air.

Zowie follows Archer as he walks through the grass, following a slight movement in the top of the grass.

ZOWIE

Archer, how far away is the Teleportee now? I'm too
short to see over this stuff.

ARCHER

Not sure. It's hard to tell scale in this grass. It could be a long ways away or close. Let's keep going.

The grass is thick and a couple of feet tall. With each step, Zowie has to reach high and stomp down on the base of the stalks to let her pass. Drops of rain land on her forehead and trickle into her eyes.

ZOWIE

Archer, it's starting to rain, and I'm kind of cold. Are you sure we're still following the Teleportee?

ARCHER

Yeah, it's OK.

Archer moves faster and faster. Zowie struggles to keep up with him.

ZOWIE

Archer, it's raining super hard. Can you even see where we are going? I can't see a thing! I don't think this is a good idea. I'm getting wet, and we could slip in this stuff and fall. You need to slow down!

Sheets of rain fly across the savannah, digging into the

ground and turning it into mud.

ZOWIE

Archer, I don't like this at all. My boots are filling with water, and I'm getting stuck in the mud!

ARCHER

Good grief, Zowie. Come on! This is so dumb. Why do you have to complain all the time? You're always just thinking of just yourself!

Zowie is much further behind Archer than before. The rain is coming down with a purpose.

ZOWIE

Archer! You aren't slowing down any!

The lightning flashes behind Zowie. A few seconds later, the boom of thunder rolls across the hidden sky above.

ZOWIE

We need to stop for a minute. I can't see anything. Archer, stop ignoring what I'm saying!

Zowie yells at Archer, who is barely visible to her in the rain.

Lightning flashes again, this time very close to Zowie, stunning her vision. She stops for a second and rubs the rain out of her eyes with fists. When she looks back at where Archer was a minute before, he is gone.

All of a sudden, Zowie is alone. Now, it seems like the world is out of control and anything could happen.

Zowie is walking and stumbling in the rain. She keeps moving forward in the same direction as before, but she can't be sure.

It's strange how hard it's raining, coming down with a passion and an intensity. Lightning streaks across the sky, but not showing anything but more rain. The thunder slams the air, making Zowie's ears ring.

She keeps going in the same direction. Her foot slips, and she tumbles down a small slope and slides through the mud.

Her suit is crumpled and muddy. Her boots are filled with water. Her face and hair are streaming with mud. And she doesn't know which way to go now.

She stops and sits down. And she waits.

And nobody comes back for her.

Then, she cries big deep sobs, gasping for breath. And all the world is like a tangled string: mixed up, confused, and hopeless.

Alone. Nobody to see her. Nobody to hear her. Nobody to understand her when she does not understand. Her thoughts are confused. She is small. A speck. A speck of alone. A speck, frozen. A speck that cannot see herself. And her head sinks lower and low.

And then, she hears the beating sound of a laugh, like a washing machine on spin cycle.

TELEPORTEE

Ha-ha-ha-ha-ha-ha-ha-ha-ha-ha-ha-ha-ha-ha-ha-ha-ha-ha-ha. You thought I was *alone*! You thought I was *helpless*! You thought I could be *used*! You thought I could be *abused*! You thought I was *yours*! You are *mine*! Ha-ha-ha-ha-ha-ha-ha-ha-ha-ha-ha-ha-ha-ha-ha-ha-ha-ha-ha.

The Teleportee is above her at the top of the hill. He is set on two sticks. The sticks are carried by two penguin aliens. Several more penguin aliens are grouped around them, standing and shifting from foot to foot, awkwardly.

Zowie pops inside her suit and comes out with the Blaster Gun. She switches a setting to the one with a picture of a lightning bolt, points it at the Teleportee, and blasts away.

VVVVVVVT!

A little spark arcs out and toward the ground but does nothing.

TELEPORTEE

Ha-ha-ha-ha-ha-ha-ha-ha-ha-ha-ha-ha-ha-ha-ha-ha-ha-ha-ha. It looks like you have the right setting but need more *power*!

Zowie drops the gun.

TELEPORTEE

Get her!

All the penguin aliens shuffle about from foot to foot, and then two of them waddle to the edge of the slope. They take out ropes with hooks at the end. They throw them down at Zowie, hooking both sides of her crumpled robot suit. They pull her up the little slope to the top, dragging her all the way. She sits there, muddy and looking very sad.

ZOWIE

I hate you, you stupid microwave!

TELEPORTEE

What you *going* to do? Kick *me*? Throw *me* over cliff?
Dumb, *selfish*, stubborn, *trash*! Rip the sleeves off! Put
her arms inside *her* suit!

The penguin aliens, almost regrettably, pull the silver
ductwork for sleeves off of her suit. They stuff her little arms
inside the rest of the suit, so she can't move them.

TELEPORTEE

Wait! Hold her!

The Teleportee pushes some buttons on his keypad.

Beep. Whrrr. Ding!

He opens up his door, reaches in, and pulls out a roll of
duct tape. He throws the roll at a penguin alien.

The penguin alien rips off strips of tape and covers each
of the armholes on Zowie's suit, pinning her inside.

TELEPORTEE

Time to take *out* the *trash*!

The two penguin aliens hold the ropes hooked to the edges of Zowie's crumpled and muddy suit and lead her away.

16.
And Archer

Meanwhile, Archer is getting angry. He is walking through the rain focused on where he wants to be. He stops, turns around and looks into the rain back toward Zowie.

ARCHER

Where is that Zowie? She is so slow! Now, I have to find her!

The wind that was behind him before slaps him in the face and fills his eyes with water.

ARCHER

Where is she? I can't see a thing!

He leans into the wind and stomps off back in the direction he had just come—he thinks. He walks for a minute or two and stops again, overcome with frustration.

ARCHER

Why does she have to go so slow and get lost, especially in this rain? Where is she?

He puts his head down and starts running, letting his anger carry him along without control for a minute. He stomps through the mud and puddles, running faster and faster, not caring which way he is going.

All of a sudden, he falls through the air.

ARCHER

Woah!

Now, Archer is sitting at the bottom of the little slope he had just fallen down. He is in a muddy hole, steep and slippery on all sides. The hole looks recently dug. Shovels are lying about inside at the bottom.

ARCHER

Uh-oh. Somebody dug a trap.

Archer looks down at the ground. The Blaster Gun is there, dropped in the mud by Zowie a minute before. It's smoking a little bit from being fired. Next to it is a half-used roll of duct tape. Zowie's boot prints are there and grooves where she was dragged through the mud up the slope.

ARCHER

Uh-oh. It's a trap for Zowie.

He sits and thinks for a second.

ARCHER

Uh-oh. The Teleportee.

He tries climbing the slope out of the little hole. He slides back down through the mud to the bottom. He tries again, harder this time, with the same result.

ARCHER

Uh-oh. Now I'm stuck in the trap.

Then, in a moment, Archer's focus changes. And he knows that he has done something very wrong.

He plops down in the mud and looks at the smoking Blaster Gun. He isn't angry at Zowie anymore, just disappointed in himself.

ARCHER

I'm an idiot.

A gust of wind blows by, and with it the rain begins to clear.

Archer sits and stares at the walls of the pit around him.

I'm not sure what Archer is thinking about. He is lost and alone inside his head.

It's funny, but you can never, never, not be where you are.

If you are stuck in the bottom of a hole and can't get out to find your friend who is in serious trouble, that is where you are right now.

If you feel guilty and disappointed in yourself because you treated your best friend very badly, that is how you feel right now.

If you don't know what to do next because it seems like the world is out of control, no matter how much you want things to be different, that is the way they are right now.

Things can change in the future, but they can't change right now.

But sometimes right now is exactly where we should be and need to be.

Archer is trying hard to accept this.

He stands up. He picks up one of the shovels from the ground. He jabs it weakly into the side of the hole. Nothing much changes. He grabs the wooden handle hard and dives the shovel into the mud with all his effort, trying to dig some steps into the side to climb out

ARCHER

Ouch! I got a splinter in my hand.

OK, I'm going to spare you the rest of this part of the story. It's pretty ugly.

But many minutes later, after much digging into the side of the hole to get himself out, Archer emerges from the pit. He is dirty and tired but peaceful.

The rain is gone now, and with it the clouds.

An earthy smell is in the air, musky and sweet, like the desert after it rains.

Archer puts the binoculars to his eyes and looks out across the savannah. He scans the horizon. He does not see a tree for a long distance.

He turns all the way around until his binoculars reach

the tower at the bottom of the valley. It's much closer now than earlier today.

ARCHER

Oh! It's the Teleportee. Oh! It's Zowie. Oh, she doesn't look so good. They're going into the door at the bottom of the tower!

17.
Reach

Archer drops the binoculars in the dirt. He doesn't need them anymore.

Now, all he has is the Blaster Gun and his permanent marker, the one he used to write the words on the microwave. He had kept it in his pocket the whole time.

He looks at the settings on the Blaster Gun. He doesn't know what they mean, so he leaves them alone.

He walks toward the tower alone.

All the trees are gone, and the land opens up into a flat ocean of grass stretching about and waving in the wind. Gently, so gently, it slopes downward toward the tower.

Now that the clouds are all gone, the sky is clear and the sun is much lower in the sky. Archer follows a little trail in the grass dug into the dirt from the pounding of many feet.

Soon, his trail joins another and gets deeper and broader.

On another trail running beside Archer's, a penguin alien trots. He carries a full trash bag in one large mitten hand. He moves ahead with purpose and speed.

The trails meet, and Archer nearly bumps into the penguin alien at the junction. The penguin alien brushes past him, ignoring him.

Soon another penguin alien, on another trail, joins the line and falls in behind Archer.

They all trot along for a while with Archer sandwiched between them.

They join other trails, each time adding one or two penguin aliens to the line.

Then, the trail takes a turn and joins a much larger and broader trail. With it, they join a crowd of about fifty penguin aliens, all moving in the same direction.

Archer is lost among a bouncing crowd of thousands of giant bellies and trash bags. The crowd of penguin aliens gets larger with each turn.

After walking for a while, the crowd slows to a crawl and gets more compressed. It inches forward step by step.

Between the bodies, Archer gets a glimpse of the tower, jumping up overhead.

It's so much larger from this angle. Made of dark stone, it strains into the sky, reaching up and getting thinner and thinner. It seems as if the tower doesn't end, turning wavy and disappearing into the sky and the giant ring around the planet.

The wind begins to blow. Instead of blowing sideways like normal wind, it blows upward. It stretches all the penguin alien hair straight up and reaching toward the sky.

And so begins the end of trash day.

Archer can see the door to the tower between penguin alien bodies.

Then, Archer steps between two penguin aliens and enters the tower. He looks up. Above him, a stone staircase spirals around and around inside the tower. It reaches up toward the top, ending in a pinhole of light far above. A line of thousands of penguin aliens climbs the stairs, each carrying a trash bag.

The wind is intense, coming from somewhere below and rushing upward through the tower.

With a penguin alien in front of him and one behind, Archer falls in and begins to climb the stairs.

. . . step, step . . .

One foot on top of the last foot. Stepping up. Each time lifting his whole weight a few inches.

. . . step, step . . .

Archer looks up at the top of the tower. Far above, the pinhole of light shines down. Is it any closer?

. . . step,

step, step, step, step, step, step, step, step, step, step, step, step, step, foible, step . . .

Rushing air flies past the staircase. Is it getting louder? The stairs keep going up and up, round and round.

Archer struggles with his thoughts. He feels trapped, claustrophobic. Stuck between two penguin aliens, climbing stairs forever. Tired and out of breath. Is he even getting any higher? He can't stop, slow down, or even speed up. His control is gone. Desperate. Panic reaches up inside of him, making his breathing even harder.

. . . step, step, step, step, step, step, step, step, step, step, step, step, step, step, step, step, step, bamboozle, step . . .

He meets a line of penguin aliens coming down the staircase. They step to the side, and it's a two-way staircase, a line going up and a line going down.

Archer is lost in time and space. He forgets where he is and where he is going. He forgets about Zowie, about the Teleportee, the planet, and home. He even stops thinking about his place and the purpose of the universe. He forgets he is tired. His body is just a machine of breathing and stepping up and up.

. . . step, macadamia, step, step, step, step, step, step, step, step, step, step, step, step, step, step, step, step, step, step, step . . .

The wind sucking upward past the staircase gets more and more intense. Archer looks up at the top of the tower. He can see that they are getting closer to the top. He can see that the pinhole of light is now a hole at the top of the inside of a cone, sucking the air upward and making it more intense.

. . . step,

step, step step . . .

This book is going to be a lot longer than I thought it would be.

. . . step, step step . . .

Finally, a door up ahead.

A few more steps and . . . the spiral staircase ends. On the left, the stairs go through a small door in the stone wall.

Archer follows the line through the door, and immediately the wind stops. The only noise is the sound of penguin alien feet and bodies. He climbs a little set of stairs and feels the open air ahead of him. He takes one last step, and he is on the top of the tower in the open air. He is standing far above the valley, level with the mountains.

The sun is setting, just a sliver of light winking behind the mountains. The moons are beginning to shine brighter, though. The moons are all grouped together above him, huddled around one spot behind the planet's ring.

The top of the tower is a platform of flat stone. It's about forty meters across in the shape of a circle with no railing around the edge.

In the middle of the platform is a transparent tube coming from below the platform and shooting straight up, up, up, and up. The tube reaches so high that the end of it can't be seen at all. It disappears into the sky and the giant ring around the whole planet.

At the bottom of the tube, near the platform, is a door just big enough for a trash bag.

Each penguin alien in the line is stepping up to the door and putting their trash bag through the door into the transparent tube. Each penguin alien watches as their trash bag is sucked straight up, up, up through the tube and into the sky, disappearing into the giant ring around the planet.

Then, each penguin alien turns around with a satisfied look, shuffles about from foot to foot in an awkward sort of way and begins the long walk back down the stairs.

Next to the tube is a group of penguin aliens without trash bags. In the middle of the group, sitting on a table with eyes glaring and long skinny arm waving about, is the Teleportee.

And, standing in the middle of all this with her arms pinned inside her suit is a scared little girl named Zowie.

18.
Terminal Velocity

Metamorphosis is a process where a creature like a dragonfly nymph or a European glass eel or a little girl will change from one thing to something different.

A caterpillar will stay inside his cocoon for a long time, going through changes he can't even see, all the time wondering who he is and what he can do.

But he can't stay inside there forever.

How does a caterpillar know when to break out of his cocoon? How does he know it's time to shed his outside layer and find out what's underneath? I don't know. I guess the caterpillar must have a little hope. Just enough hope to see himself as being more than a caterpillar.

It's a good thing to get a real glimpse of who you are from the outside. To see things about yourself that you could never see with a mirror. It's good to like who that is.

The Teleportee sits on his table and thinks. He thinks about his past. The creatures and things he has met. The creatures and things he has communicated with. The creatures and things he wants to meet again. The creatures and things he wants to destroy.

The Teleportee waves his cord about in an easy and relaxed sort of way. He is finally feeling comfortable with the way things are.

The crowd of penguin aliens stands and shuffles from foot to foot in a listening sort of way.

TELEPORTEE

Let's *talk* about an idea we *call dumb*, selfish, stubborn . . . and *trash*!

Beep, beep, beep.

Beep. Whrrr. Ding!

The Teleportee reaches inside himself and produces a dictionary. Then, he waves it around in the air for a minute with his cord.

TELEPORTEE

The dictionary defines *dumb* as 1) Having not much *thinking* going on up there and 2) the Zowie Girl. It defines *selfish* as 1) Thinking about *yourself* too much, and 2) the Zowie Girl. It defines *stubborn* as 1) Doesn't want to do what reasonable creatures and *the Teleportee* want it to *do*, and 2) the Zowie Girl. It defines trash as 1) stuff we don't want because it is *useless* and to be put in the *trash tube* and 2) *the Zowie Girl*! Penguin aliens, put the *Zowie* Girl in the *trash tube*! Suck her out into the vast *expanse* and *vacuum of space*!

ARCHER

Not today!

Archer fires the Blaster Gun at the Teleportee.

VVVVVVTTT!

TELEPORTEE

Ha-ha-ha-ha-ha-ha-ha-ha-ha-ha-ha-ha-ha-ha-ha. Same *old* problem. Same *Blaster Gun*, not enough *power*! Penguin aliens, grab that *Archer Boy*! Throw his *Blaster Gun* on the *floor*!

ARCHER

Argh! Let go, you stupid penguin aliens. Why are you doing what that stupid Teleportee is telling you to do? It doesn't make sense!

TELEPORTEE

Put the *Zowie* Girl in the tube! *Now*!

Archer is helpless, both his arms held by a penguin alien. He looks at a scared Zowie.

The two penguin aliens holding Zowie begin to drag her by her suit over to the door to the trash tube.

Zowie looks down at the cardboard suit she is pinned inside. She used to love her robot costume with its silver paint, buttons, knobs, and other shiny bits all placed in such a happy way. But now it is a crumpled mass of cardboard, caked in dirt, gravel, and all the broken bits.

Zowie knows that it's time to shed this outside layer and find out what's underneath.

ARCHER

You can do it, Zowie. You can do it. I know you can.

Zowie struggles inside her suit. A fight on the inside, a fight hidden from the world.

ZOWIE

Grrrrrrraaaaaaaarrrrraaarrr!!!!!!

ARCHER

Come on, Zowie!

ZOWIE

Eeeeeeeooooaaaa!

Zowie busts out of her suit. Bits and pieces of muddy cardboard, baby carrots, chewing gum, a headlamp, and mobile phone fly in all directions.

Here is Zowie without her robot costume. She stands confidently. She is wearing what she had on underneath all along, a grey hoodie on top with a purple skirt below and her short little legs shoot out the bottom covered in jeans.

Zowie runs over to the Blaster Gun, lying on the stone platform. She knows what to do with it. She understands how it works, now. She twists its power setting up to ten.

The Teleportee sees the look in Zowie's eyes, full of confidence and determination. He swings his power cord arm around wildly and launches himself off of the table and on to the floor. He digs his power cord into the slippery stone floor and scuttles away from Zowie desperately.

TELEPORTEE

No! Must go now! Must go back to above refrigerator!

The Teleportee bumps into a penguin alien foot, flips over it, and his door pops open. His cord waves around helplessly.

Zowie points the Blaster Gun at the Teleportee and pulls the trigger.

VVVVVTTT!

With a shower of sparks, the Teleportee slides across the stone platform of the tower, coming to a stop at the very edge.

The eyes of the Teleportee go dead. The Teleportee is gone. It is just a microwave again.

At that moment, the last penguin alien comes up the stairs puts his trash bag in the trash tube. And with it, the wind whistling up the tower and through the tube stops.

The sun's eye winks closed behind the mountains.

And now, just as always happens as the sun disappears for the day, a small push of breeze blows over them.

Scrrrapppe!!!

The dead microwave teeters over the edge of the platform, about to fall off the tower.

ARCHER

Uh-oh!

Archer runs and dives for the microwave. He grabs the cord just as it tips over the edge of the platform. It falls, and Archer slides with it over the side of the tower.

ARCHER

Come on, Zowie. It's time to go!

Zowie runs and dives headfirst over the edge of the tower, too.

ZOWIE

Did you see me? Did you see me? I busted out of my
wrapper just like *The Very Hungry Caterpillar*! And now
I'm flying like a butterfly!

ARCHER

You were awesome! You saved the day!

ZOWIE

I'm sorry we didn't get to go to the star you wanted to
today.

ARCHER

This was pretty much what I wanted to do, anyway. I'm
sorry for leaving you alone.

ZOWIE

I got to see myself today! I got to see a what kind of a
girl I am! I saw just what I can do. I'm a *warrior*!

ARCHER

You *are* a warrior! You fought the Teleportee and killed
him. You were the most important person today.

ZOWIE

Really? What happens next?

ARCHER

I don't know. It has been real fun, though.

ZOWIE

I know. I'm sorry I kicked you in the butt. Can we do this tomorrow?

ARCHER

Yes. But I'm kind of hungry and want to go home now.

ZOWIE

Me too!

Archer, Zowie, and the microwave all fall together through the air. They plummet downward at terminal velocity, but the ground is still a very long ways away. They are weightless, suspended in the moment.

Archer reaches into his pocket and pulls out the permanent marker.

He grabs onto the falling microwave and begins to write.

He rubs out one letter from the word TELEPORTEE.

Then, he draws a new letter.

Now, the microwave says TELEPORTER.

ARCHER

A Teleportee receives, but a Teleporter sends.

Archer pushes some buttons.

Beep, beep, beep.

Beep. Whrrr. Ding!

Archer opens the door and motions for Zowie.

Zowie squirms into the doorway of the open Teleporter.

Her legs stick out of the door for a moment, then she disappears inside.

Archer follows.

His hand reaches out to close the door.

The empty Teleporter falls through the air for a minute.

Then, it crashes into the ground, flying into a thousand pieces.

Somewhere in the Milky Way Galaxy, there is a little blue-green planet called Earth.

On that planet, there is a pile of hills. They are covered in grass and sprinkled with trees.

Winding down from these hills is a path.

And on that path, just past the traversable wormhole that closed behind them, are two hungry friends, Archer and Zowie.

The End

Made in the USA
Lexington, KY
06 November 2019

56658848R00153